"You've come back. It's about time, don't you think?"

"About time?" Dr. Brett Elliot hadn't expected his hometown to stage a welcome parade to celebrate his return. But he also hadn't expected to be accosted by a beautiful woman he'd never met. "Ms.—"

"You don't know who I am?"

"You're not…?"

Something about her amber eyes triggered recognition. He brushed back her auburn curls, exposing a thin scar. She'd fallen from a tree when she was five, and he'd been convinced at ten he was grown up enough to take care of her. That was when he'd decided to become a doctor.

"Rebecca. Little Rebecca, all grown up."

"People do, you know. Did you think nothing in Bedford Creek would change while you were gone, that we were all just waiting for your return?"

Rebecca had been a quiet little tomboy, all skinny legs and sharp elbows. The woman who stood in front of him now was beautiful.

"I guess things *have* changed," Brett said, lifting an eyebrow.

Books by Marta Perry

Love Inspired

A Father's Promise #41
Since You've Been Gone #75
*Desperately Seeking Dad #91
The Doctor Next Door #104

*Hometown Heroes

MARTA PERRY

began writing children's stories for Sunday school take-home papers when she was a church education director. From that beginning she branched into writing magazine fiction and then book-length fiction. She's grateful for the opportunity to write the books of her heart for Steeple Hill.

Marta lives in rural Pennsylvania with her husband of thirty-eight years. They have three grown children scattered around the globe whom they enjoy visiting. In addition to writing and travel, Marta loves hearing from readers and responding to their letters. You can write to her at Steeple Hill Books, 300 East 42nd St., New York, NY 10017.

The Doctor Next Door
Marta Perry

Love Inspired®

Published by Steeple Hill Books™

STEEPLE HILL BOOKS

Steeple Hill™

ISBN 0-373-87110-4

THE DOCTOR NEXT DOOR

Copyright © 2000 by Martha Johnson

Visit us at www.steeplehill.com

Printed in U.S.A.

For we are God's workmanship,
created in Christ Jesus to do good works,
which God prepared in advance for us to do.
                              —*Ephesians* 2:10

This book is dedicated to the dear writing friends and critique partners who kept me going all these years: Barbara, Andi, Laurie, Dave and Pam. And, as always, to Brian.

Chapter One

‸

"**Y**ou've come back."

The young woman's golden-brown eyes filled with a mix of shock and some other emotion Brett couldn't identify.

She grabbed his arm, pulling him out of the flow of people coming through the front door of the gracious Victorian home. "It's about time, don't you think?"

"About time?" Dr. Brett Elliot hadn't expected his hometown to stage a welcome parade to celebrate his return. But he also hadn't expected to be accosted at his best friend's engagement party by a beautiful woman he'd never seen before.

There'd been no mistaking the sarcasm in her voice. "The party started at eight, didn't it?" He detached his arm from her grip. People clustered in

the adjoining rooms, leaving the wide center hallway quiet.

"The party? Yes." She glanced toward the
crowded living room of the rambling old house,
where the party obviously centered. Auburn hair
curled around her shoulders; creamy skin glowed
against the soft coral of her dress.

No, if he'd known this woman before, he'd certainly remember.

"Well, then, I'm right on time." He probably
wouldn't have ventured out at all on his first night
back in Bedford Creek if he weren't one of Mitch's
groomsmen. He could hardly avoid the party given
for Mitch and Anne, especially since it was at the
Forrester place, right next door to his parents'
empty house. Apparently one of the Forrester sisters
was a member of the wedding party.

He couldn't pretend he hadn't gotten home for
it. Someone would notice his car or the light in the
window. That was one of the drawbacks he remembered of life in a small town. Someone noticed everything.

So he had decided to make a brief appearance,
smile at everyone and beat a quick retreat before
too many questions were asked.

Nothing in that scenario included having a
stranger look at him with such disapproval. He
pushed down his annoyance and tried a smile.
"You think I should have come early, Ms.—"

Her eyebrows went up in astonishment. "You don't know who I am?"

He riffled quickly through his mental file of high school friends. Trouble was, he hadn't come back to Pennsylvania often during college and medical school on the West Coast. He was much closer since he'd taken the residency at a Philadelphia hospital, but also much busier. And with his parents spending most of the year in Florida, there'd been little to bring him back. People had a way of changing when you didn't see them for years at a time.

"Well, let's see. You must be someone I went to school with, right?"

A dimple showed at the corner of her mouth, dissipating her frown. "In a way."

The smile encouraged him. She couldn't be that annoyed with him, even if he'd gotten the time wrong. Something about her made him think of Angela Forrester, his high school sweetheart. One of Angela's friends, maybe?

"Were you a cheerleader, like Angela?"

"No." Her amber eyes seemed to enjoy a secret laugh at his expense.

"You're not..."

Something about her eyes triggered recognition. He brushed the auburn curls back from her cheek, exposing the hairline-thin white scar.

She'd fallen from the willow tree in the backyard when she was five. He'd been the first person there, and he'd held the hem of his T-shirt over the cut, convinced that at ten he was grown up enough to take care of her. That might have been the moment he'd decided to become a doctor.

"Rebecca." Now that he realized, of course, it could be no one else. "Little Rebecca, all grown up."

She drew back casually from his touch. "People do, you know."

He shook his head. "It's impossible. You used to look like Orphan Annie, all frizzy red hair and big eyes."

Now she was beautiful. The idea stunned him. How could Angela's pesky kid sister look like this?

"Gee, thanks. I think."

"I didn't mean..." He was thrown ridiculously off balance. Of course Rebecca had grown up. She couldn't stay little forever.

"You expected me to look like a kid. Did you think nothing in Bedford Creek would change while you were gone, that we were all just waiting for your return? It's not Brigadoon, you know."

"Isn't it?" They'd done "Brigadoon" for their senior class play. Angela had been gorgeous in a tartan skirt. Somehow Bedford Creek had always had that Brigadoon aura—isolated, hidden by its mountains, remote from his busy urban life.

"Things do change. I grew up. Angela got engaged. You can't just walk back in and find everything the way you left it."

The edge in her voice startled him. Rebecca had

been a quiet little tomboy, all skinny legs and sharp elbows. She'd tagged after him and Angela, always wanting to be just like them, until it nearly drove Angela crazy.

"I guess things *have* changed." He lifted an eyebrow. "Way I remember it, you'd no more have argued with anyone than you'd have flown off the roof."

She smiled, the flicker of antagonism disappearing, at least for the moment. "I think I did try to fly off the porch once, using Mom's tablecloth for a cape."

"So you did. Are you still a tomboy?" Teasing Rebecca felt like old times, and the tension he'd been carrying around for weeks seemed to slide away. "Still falling out of willow trees?"

"Not anymore." Her chin lifted, perhaps with pride. "I'm a physician's assistant now. I work with Dr. Overton at the clinic."

The mention of his old mentor's name jolted something inside him. He had to see Clifford Overton soon, but he already dreaded the encounter. Doc would have to be told what had happened to Brett's fellowship. And Doc would have expectations of his own about Brett's future.

"How is Doc?"

A troubled look crossed her face, dimming the sparkle of her eyes. "Getting old." She shook her head, as if shaking away something she didn't want to think about. "He'll be excited to see you. You haven't been in touch enough.'' She pinned him down with a straightforward look he remembered from the little girl she'd been. ''You are here to stay, aren't you?''

Something tightened painfully inside him. Stay? Was that the only choice left to him? He rejected that quickly. With the end of his residency he'd lost his student apartment, so coming to Bedford Creek was the logical thing to do. But as soon as he found a new fellowship, he'd be gone.

When he didn't answer, Rebecca's intent gaze seemed to bore into his very soul. ''That is why you've come back, isn't it? To take over the clinic from Doc, the way he's always planned?''

''Not exactly.''

Coming to the Forresters had been a mistake. He should have waited to read about the party on the social page of *The Chronicle*. What gave Rebecca the right to put him on the spot?

''Then why are you in town?'' The edge was back in her voice.

For an instant he wanted to spill the whole story and get it off his chest. The thought horrified him. Nobody needed to know Brett Elliot, M.D., once the pride of Bedford Creek High School, had sacrificed the prestigious fellowship his mother had probably bragged about in every letter to her friends.

''Just on a break.'' He took a step back. It was time little Rebecca stopped interrogating him—time he congratulated Mitch and Anne and then got out of here.

"A break?" She stared at him in disbelief. "What do you mean, 'a break'? Doc's been waiting for you to come back."

He fought down a wave of anger. "That's between Doc and me."

She didn't seem to agree. "You have an obligation here, remember? A debt to pay."

Her challenge stung, reminding him of too much he wasn't ready to face yet. "My debts don't concern you, Rebecca."

"Everything about the clinic concerns me." She shot the words back at him. They were suddenly on opposite sides of a chasm, glaring at each other.

"Look, if you think…" The rest of that sentence vanished when someone bolted through the archway from the living room and flung herself into his arms.

Memories flooded him. The same perfume, the same clinging hands, the same soft voice chattering a mile a minute. *Angela.*

"Brett! I thought I heard your voice, but I didn't believe it. I'm so glad to see you, I just can't believe you're here." She threw her arms around his neck, half choking him.

He tried to disentangle himself, but Angela's words had pierced the din in the living room. In a moment he was surrounded.

He wasn't going to escape the party in the foreseeable future. And over Angela's head he saw Rebecca waiting, apparently ready to demand the answers he didn't intend to give.

Tension tightened Rebecca's nerves as she took a step back from the flurry of greetings. The quarrel that had flared up between her and Brett had taken her completely by surprise, and she needed a moment to think.

A cold hand clutched her heart. Brett couldn't be backing out of his agreement. He couldn't. She longed to push her sister out of the way, grab Brett's arm and demand that he explain himself.

Lord, what's happening here? We've waited so long for Brett to come back. You know how much Doc needs him, how much this town needs him. Doesn't he know that?

The middle of Mitch and Anne's party was no place for a confrontation. Still, she felt the rush of unasked questions pressing on her lips as if determined to get out.

She took a deep breath and pasted a smile on her face. She'd known the instant Brett walked in that his presence meant trouble. She'd seen him and felt as if someone had punched her right in the heart.

She pushed the thought away. Her long-ago feelings for Brett had been childish adoration, that was all. Not love. She'd been a kid. She hadn't known what love was.

Mitch Donovan had reached Brett, grabbing his

hand to shake it, and Brett's face lit with pleasure at the sight of his old friend. Rebecca took the opportunity to get a good look at Brett, one uncolored by shock at seeing him after all these years.

Some things hadn't changed. His hair, the color of antique gold, still fell, unruly, over his broad forehead. Green-as-glass eyes warmed as he hugged Anne Morden, Mitch's fiancée. He was taller and broader than she remembered—his shoulders filled out the dark wool blazer he wore—and his skin was still tanned, even though it was fall.

He still had that cleft chin, of course, and his smile was the one that had devastated the girls of Bedford Creek High. It had probably devastated quite a few women since, too.

Everyone wanted to talk to Brett, the local boy who'd made good. People were proud tiny Bedford Creek High had produced a graduate who'd gone to one of the best medical schools in the country, and Brett's mother had never let an opportunity pass to tell people how well he'd been doing.

Rebecca could slip away, unnoticed, out of the range of that smile and the memories it evoked.

She crossed the center hall to the dining room, trying to concentrate on the buffet. The cherry table had all its leaves in to accommodate the food her mother had insisted on. The moment she'd learned Rebecca was going to be Anne's bridesmaid, she'd begun planning the party, maybe considering it a trial run for the parties that would accompany Angela's wedding next spring.

Rebecca checked the platters, listening to the buzz of conversation, and frowned a little. Was she the only one who noticed a faint shadow in Brett's eyes when the subject of his Philadelphia residency came up? Maybe so. Or maybe she was imagining things in the flow of chatter and good humor and congratulations.

She'd thought at the time he took the residency that he should have come home instead. After all, Doc had helped Brett's family pay for his medical-school education when they'd had a struggle to meet tuition payments. He'd helped other young people, too, but Brett was different. He'd always expected that one day Brett would take over his practice. They'd planned it together, and the only reason Rebecca knew was because she worked so closely with Doc.

But the years had slipped away. Whenever she brought it up, Doc was philosophical. Let Brett take the residency, he'd said. It would make him a better doctor when he did come back.

Well, now he was home, but apparently not to stay. Her throat tightened. She hadn't realized how much she'd been counting on his return until she saw him. How much longer could they continue at the clinic if he didn't take over? The secret Doc insisted she keep weighed on her heart. If only she could share it with Brett—

"There you are." Brett touched her arm, and the cake platter tilted in her grasp. He grabbed it, setting it down. "Anne sent me over to tell you to relax and enjoy the party. There's plenty of food here. More fat and calories than this bunch should have in a month."

She managed a smile. *Keep it light. You can't confront him here, so keep it light.* "You're back in Bedford Creek, remember? A party isn't a success unless the hostess stuffs everyone."

"Nobody serves crudités and yogurt dip?"

"Not unless they're serving fudge and cookies with it."

This was better, joking back and forth with Brett as if it were the old days, burying her worries about the clinic, about Doc, about the future. And ignoring the tingle of awareness his closeness brought. She had to keep things on this level for the moment.

She tried unobtrusively to move a step farther away. Ignoring his warmth and strength would be easier if he weren't quite so close to her, close enough to smell a faint trace of spicy aftershave, close enough to see the gold flecks in his green eyes.

"Anne tells me you're a bridesmaid in the wedding next month."

She nodded. It was safe to talk about Anne. "We've gotten to be good friends since she moved here. She's really someone special." The secret of Emilie's birth parents had brought Anne to Bedford

Creek, but it was the love she'd found with Mitch that made her stay.

She looked at Anne, bending to disentangle Emilie's tiny fingers from the bow of a present. She admired Anne's cool urban elegance without wanting to be like her.

He followed the direction of her gaze. "They are happy, aren't they?" He almost sounded as if he needed assurance.

"Of course." Her surprise showed in her voice. "They're perfect for each other. Don't you think so?"

He glanced down at her. "Guess I never thought Mitch would settle down. But once he met the right woman, it was all over for him."

She couldn't help but smile. "You make it sound like a prison sentence. Is that how you see marriage?"

"It is meant to be permanent."

He looked back toward the other room, and she realized he was watching Alex Caine, the third member of the trio of friends. Alex, his lean face serious as always, stood back a little, leaning on the cane he sometimes had to use.

"Alex is doing better." She answered the question he didn't ask. Alex had barely survived a plane crash the year before, suffering a head injury that eventually healed and a shattered knee that still pained him. It was small wonder his friends worried about him.

Brett nodded. "Alex is tough—nobody knows that better than I do. He'll be fine." He focused on her. "So how come I haven't heard about an engagement party for you? Guys must be standing in line."

"In Bedford Creek?" She lifted her brows. "There aren't enough eligible single guys to form a line."

"Don't give me that. You ought to be wearing a ring, too."

She shook her head. "Always a bridesmaid, never a bride. That's the way I like it, although I'll never convince my mother. She's eternally hopeful of getting both her daughters married off."

"She must—" Brett interrupted himself to look down. "Did you know there was someone under the table?"

She bent, lifting the hem of the linen tablecloth. "Come out, Kristie. Come on, right now."

A small, sticky hand closed around hers, and her niece slid out from under the table. Chocolate smeared Kristie's hands and mouth.

"Who's this?" Brett knelt beside the pajama-clad figure. "I haven't met you before, have I?"

Finger in her mouth, five-year-old Kristie had an attack of shyness. She leaned against Rebecca's skirt, shaking her head.

Brett looked up, a question in his eyes.

"Kristie is Quinn's daughter." It was useless to hope he wouldn't ask more questions. He and

Quinn were the same age, and they'd been childhood friends. "Honey, this is Brett. He's an old friend."

"I don't think I knew your brother had come back home." Brett stood. "My mother's intelligence-gathering skills must be getting rusty."

"He's not. Home, that is." Her heart ached at the thought of her brother's battle with grief over his wife's death six months earlier. "He's finishing up a job. Kristie is staying with us until he comes back."

Brett seemed to process very quickly all the things she didn't say. He smiled down at Kristie. "Sounds like you're a lucky girl, staying with your grandma and aunts. Is there still a tree house in the willow out back?"

Kristie nodded. "Aunt Rebecca and me painted it. It's yellow now."

"I'd like to see that sometime. Do you let boys in?"

That earned a shy smile. "You're not a boy."

"I'm not?" He gave her a shocked look.

"You're a man!" She erupted in giggles, and he joined her.

Brett had made another conquest, not surprisingly. He always had been able to charm the birds from the trees. And there was genuine kindness behind his smile. Small wonder even shy Kristie responded to it, just as Rebecca had.

She must have been about her niece's age when

she'd solemnly asked Brett if he'd marry her when she grew up. They'd been in the tree house, and she could still smell the lilacs that had been blooming in the garden.

Brett had been kind; he was always kind. He'd taken both her hands in his and assured her she'd meet someone she'd love lots more than him. He was going to be a doctor, he'd told her. He promised he'd come back and take care of all of them.

She'd tried to blink tears away, knowing a rejection when she heard it, even at five. She'd nodded, as if accepting his words, but her heart had known she loved him.

Now, she could only hope Brett had forgotten that embarrassing incident.

"Come on." She took Kristie's hand. "Time we got you back to bed."

At least that would get her out of Brett's company for a few minutes. She wouldn't have to pretend nothing was wrong, and she wouldn't have to pretend she wasn't affected by seeing him again.

Kristie's curly red head burrowed against her skirt. "I'm tired, Auntie Rebecca. Carry me."

Brett scooped her up before Rebecca could move. "I'll take her."

"Wait, let me wipe off the chocolate." She snatched a napkin. "You don't need to do that. You should stay here and visit with people."

She hoped there wasn't a desperate edge in her

voice. The last thing she wanted right now was to be alone with him.

He ignored her. "Here we go." He hoisted Kristie, hands now clean, to his shoulder. "Hold on tight." He started for the archway, bouncing her so that she giggled and clutched his hair.

Managing a meaningless smile for anyone who might be watching, Rebecca followed.

They trooped up the wide staircase. At the top, she nodded toward the door next to hers. "This is Kristie's room."

"Duck your head, Kristie." He stooped under the door frame, earning another giggle, and plopped Kristie on the white single bed with its bright quilt. "Ready for bed."

"Wound up, you mean." Rebecca pulled back the quilt. "In you go, and say your prayers. It's way past bedtime, and you have school tomorrow, remember?"

Kristie pouted. "Don't want to go to bed. Don't want to go to school." She bounced. "I want to stay at the party."

Rebecca could read the warning signs of a disturbed night. "Kristie..."

Brett sat down on the edge of the bed. "You're not going to tell me this girl goes to school, are you? What are you...fifth grade? Sixth?"

Kristie giggled, not seeming to notice that he was putting her down on the pillow, tucking the quilt around her. "I'm in kindergarten."

"Wow!" He managed a suitable look of surprise as he clicked off the bedside lamp, leaving the room bathed in the soft glow of the night-light. "So how do you like kindergarten?"

"Okay, I guess." She looked down. "Sometimes Jeffy takes my crayons. And he says I'm a…a carrottop." She said the word as if it were monstrous.

Rebecca's throat tightened. She'd known something was wrong at school, but Kristie had been stubbornly uncommunicative about it. Now she'd blurted it out to Brett on the basis of a five-minute acquaintanceship.

"Do you know what a carrottop is?" Brett smoothed her red curls.

She nodded solemnly. "Grandma had some carrots in her garden."

Brett lifted a springy strand of red. "I'll bet she did, but Jeffy was talking about your hair. Because he thinks it's the color of a carrot." He glanced up at Rebecca, smiling. "Aunt Rebecca had hair this color when she was your age, and I always thought it was the prettiest hair color in the world. Maybe Jeffy thinks so, too."

Rebecca's heart gave a ridiculous *thump*. He was talking nonsense to soothe Kristie, of course. She couldn't let it affect her. Couldn't let it bring back sharp, evocative images of a much younger Brett. He wasn't that person anymore. And she wasn't that little girl.

"But he teases me."

"I'll tell you a secret." Brett leaned close to the child and lowered his voice to a whisper. "Boys only tease girls they like." He looked up at her again, eyes laughing. "Isn't that right, Aunt Rebecca?"

She kept smiling by sheer effort of will, heart thumping. "That's right."

She wasn't the child who'd idolized him any longer. But she'd have to do something about the ridiculous way her heart turned over every time he smiled at her.

Chapter Two

Memories assailed Brett as he poured a mug of coffee in the sunny kitchen of his parents' house the next morning. Memories of himself and Angela, back when she'd been the most important person in his world. He had to smile now at that infatuation. Angela didn't seem to have grown up at all since then. It was Rebecca whose maturity astounded him.

Mitch and Alex hadn't changed, though.

He smiled, thinking of them, but a shadow tinged his mind. He could keep his problems a secret from most people, but he couldn't withhold them from Alex and Mitch.

Still, their support was one thing he knew he could always count on, no matter what. The three of them had faced death together, once upon a time. That had created a bond nothing could break.

His mind drifted back to the party the night before. Rebecca had been right—Mitch and Anne really were meant for each other. The fact that they'd be starting married life with a ready-made family of her adopted baby and his foster son just seemed to add to their glow.

Alex was another story. Brett frowned down at his cup. Alex might be able to hide his pain from other people, but not from him. He'd give anything for a look at Alex's medical charts. He owed Alex—owed him a lot. If there was a way he could make up for the past, he'd like to find it.

He put down the coffee. Somehow everything—every concern, every conversation, even every thought, led him straight to the clinic. Rebecca was probably wondering why he wasn't there already, and she wouldn't hesitate to tell him so. If he'd known pesky little Rebecca would turn into such a beautiful, determined young woman, maybe he'd have stayed in touch.

Or maybe he'd have avoided her like the plague.

He didn't owe Rebecca an explanation, regardless of whether she agreed. But he certainly owed one to Doc, easy or not—and it was time he paid him a visit.

He drove out to the corner, then turned uphill. In Bedford Creek you were always going either up the mountain or down toward the river. There wasn't anything between. The town was wedged tightly into the narrow valley, with mountain ridges hemming it in.

The new tourist brochures his mother had sent him described Bedford Creek and its mountains as the Switzerland of Pennsylvania. People had obviously tried to live up to that billing, decking houses with colorful shutters and window boxes. Now, the boxes overflowed with marigolds and mums.

Apparently the publicity campaign was working. Strangers slinging cameras dotted the sidewalks, and a line waited to board the old-fashioned steam train for a jaunt through the mountains to see the autumn foliage. In another week or two the woods would be in full color, and the place jammed.

Doc Overton's clinic sat at the top of the hill, its faded red brick looking just the same as it always had. Brett's first glimpse of the familiar white clapboard sign swamped him in a wave of nostalgia. He pulled into the gravel lot and got out of the car slowly.

What had led to that promise he'd once made Rebecca about becoming a doctor? One of those early visits, when Doc thumped him and patted his head and told him he was fine? Or when Doc had responded to the interest he'd shown in some procedure, taking the time to explain it to him? Whenever it had been, Doc Overton had certainly been part of it.

It had been too long since he'd been back, too long since he'd let Doc know how much he appreciated his mentoring. That had to be a part of the talk they needed to have. He took the two steps to the porch and opened the door.

New wallpaper decked a waiting room that was far more crowded than he ever remembered it being. It looked as if he'd have to postpone their conversation. Clearly Doc wouldn't have time for a talk this morning—not with all these patients waiting.

He didn't intend to rush this conversation. Telling Doc the changes he wanted to make to the future they had once planned wouldn't be easy.

Maybe the best course was to see Doc and arrange a time when they could be alone, uninterrupted. He exchanged greetings with people he knew as he edged his way to the desk.

He nodded to the receptionist, wondering if she was someone he should remember. "I'm Dr. Elliot. I'd like a word with Dr. Overton when he has a moment."

"Brett." Rebecca appeared from behind the rows of files, looking startled. "I didn't expect to see you so soon."

He lifted an eyebrow. "Funny. I got the impression I'd better show my face around here pretty quickly or someone might get after me. Can't imagine why I thought that."

A warm flush brightened her peaches-and-cream complexion. "I can't either." She gestured toward the hallway. "Come on back."

The treatment area had changed even more than

the waiting room. Cream paint unified it, and a modern counter had replaced the old rolltop desk where Doc had once kept a jumble of papers. Charts were neatly filed, and an up-to-date computer system ruled the countertop.

He stopped, assessing the changes, then turned to Rebecca. She'd changed, too. Her bronze hair was tied back from her face, and a matching bronze name pin adorned her neat uniform. Everything about her spoke of efficiency and professionalism. How strange to see little Rebecca so grown-up and businesslike.

"Were you responsible for all this?" He gestured toward the changes, knowing old Doc wouldn't have modernized a thing if someone hadn't pushed him into it.

She looked startled. "I guess I did suggest we were due for some up-to-date touches."

"You mean you nagged him until it was easier to say yes." He smiled at her. "Don't fib to me, Rebecca. I know both of you too well."

"Something like that." She smiled back, but there was a shadow behind it. She was probably still thinking about their unfinished conversation the night before—

"There you are."

The familiar voice sounded behind Brett, and he swung around.

"About time you were getting back here to see us."

"Hasn't been that long, has it?" He gripped Doc's hand, emotion flooding him. It *had* been too long. Rebecca had been right. Doc Overton was getting old.

The hair he remembered as iron gray was white now, and Doc's shoulders stooped, as if he'd spent too many years carrying all the medical burdens of the town. The lines in his face formed a road map of wisdom and caring.

"Come here, boy." Not content with a handshake, Doc pulled him close for a quick hug, then pounded his shoulder. "Good to see you. How are they treating you at that big city hospital?"

There was the question he didn't want to answer, and it was the first one out of Doc's mouth, of course.

"Things are going okay." He managed a smile. "It was tough getting used to Philly after all those years in California."

"Not enough beaches, huh?" Those wise old eyes surveyed him. "If you want to succeed in this business, you have to make some sacrifices."

"Like having any time for yourself," Rebecca said. She held out a chart. "I'm sorry to interrupt the reunion, but you're running about an hour behind already."

"Doc always runs an hour behind," Brett said. That was probably because Doc had never heard the notion that the physician should spend only ten of his precious minutes with any single patient. And if he heard it, he'd dismiss it. He knew his patients too well to rush anyone out of the office. When you were closeted with Doc Overton, you felt as if you were the most important person in the world to him. "Don't people still set their clocks by him?"

Rebecca smiled, but it was more an automatic response than an agreement. "I'm afraid people are a bit more impatient than they used to be."

Doc shrugged, lifting his hands. "What can I do? This young woman runs the place, and she runs me, too. We'll have to get together later."

"How about supper tonight? We can catch up." And talk about the future.

Doc nodded. "Sounds good, if I get out of here at a decent hour. I'll call you."

"I'll see you later, then." He should be ashamed at the relief he felt over putting off the difficult conversation.

"Why don't you stay and help out?" Rebecca's voice stopped him before he took a step toward the door. "You're licensed in Pennsylvania, aren't you? You could see some of Doc's overflow and let him get through by lunchtime for once."

"You think people really want to consult a doctor they knew when he was a kid?" His reluctance surprised him. Maybe it was the thought of treating people he knew so well—people who'd watched him grow up.

"Don't worry about it." Rebecca gave him a

challenging look. "They accept me as a professional, believe it or not. They'll listen to you."

His gaze clashed with hers. She'd made her attitude clear last night, even though they hadn't had a chance to talk about it again. She thought it was time he took over for Doc, and she probably couldn't imagine there might be something better than a one-doctor practice, either for the town or for him.

"Good idea." Doc nodded. "Let folks see a real city doctor for once."

Brett forced a smile. He wasn't about to let little Rebecca push him into saying anything to Doc about his plans in front of her, if that was in her mind. But he could hardly walk away with Doc looking at him so expectantly.

"Sure. I'll be glad to see some patients."

He caught the satisfied look on Rebecca's face, and his jaw tightened. Rebecca might have won this round, but if she thought she could manipulate him into doing what she wanted, she'd better think again.

Was her plan going to work? The question kept revolving in Rebecca's mind while she found a lab coat for Brett, showed him the examining rooms, led him through her system.

She hadn't been able to sleep after the party, her mind constantly returning to Brett. What had he meant when he'd said he was just home on a break?

Didn't he realize how much Doc needed him? How much all of Bedford Creek needed him?

It had taken her longer than it should have to realize she needed to pray about it. Even then, she'd found herself wrestling with the situation, trying fruitlessly to see an immediate solution.

Finally, exhausted, she'd left it in the Lord's hands and gone to sleep. And when she woke, the answer seemed so clear.

Brett wouldn't listen to her, and he certainly wouldn't let her tell him what to do. But if she showed him how desperately Doc needed him, he'd do the right thing, wouldn't he?

Doubt gripped her. The idealistic boy she'd known would have. She wasn't so sure about the sophisticated stranger he'd become.

Well, doing something was better than doing nothing. The opportunity to show Brett how much he was needed had come. She had to take advantage of it.

"If you're all set, I'll just see which of the patients would be willing to switch to you."

Brett raised an eyebrow. "Don't you mean, would agree to be fobbed off on the new guy?"

It was going to be tough to keep a professional distance, she thought, if he persisted in looking at her with that devastating smile. "I'm sure there won't be a problem. I'll just try to keep everyone happy." She shuffled rapidly through the charts.

"Is that your main objective in life?"

The question caught her by surprise. "What do you mean?"

He leaned against the counter next to her. "Keeping everyone happy. You seem to do a lot of that." He gestured at the renovated office. "You're certainly keeping Doc happy. And making a difference here. Is that why you chose a medical career?"

"I..." She bit back the response that sprang to her lips, shocked at her impulse to tell him he was responsible for that decision. That was something Brett didn't need to know about her. "I guess, in a way. Doc needs help, and it's not easy to find qualified medical personnel who want to come to a small town and work in a one-doctor clinic."

"So you felt it was your duty?"

He really seemed to want to understand. "It wasn't just that. My family's here, and after Dad died, they needed me."

The familiar picture formed in her mind. Her father, his face lined and tired, grasping her hand in his. *You're the responsible one, Rebecca. You'll have to take care of them.*

Brett nodded, but she could see the question still in his eyes.

"There are plenty of opportunities for physician's assistants these days," he said. "You could go almost anywhere."

"I'm happy here." Why did he assume that just because *he* couldn't wait to leave Bedford Creek, other people felt that way? "Not everyone's destined for the medical fast track."

He gave her a wary look. "Is that aimed at me, by any chance?"

She wouldn't get anywhere by antagonizing him. "No, of course not." She picked up a chart. "Are you ready for the first patient?"

His gaze probed for a moment, as if he tried to see into her thoughts.

Finally he nodded. "Bring them on. I'm ready."

She put Minna Dawson's chart in Brett's stack and showed him to an exam room. Chronic indigestion—and Minna was anxious to get back to the shop. She'd agree to see Brett if that meant moving her appointment up.

Doc fell further behind with every patient; everyone knew that. But everyone didn't know how tired he was. They didn't see the little lapses she'd been vigilant at catching and correcting.

Tension knotted her stomach. Doc had to have help, and soon. If only Doc would be honest about how much he needed Brett.

As she took histories for the other patients, did preliminary work-ups, and moved smoothly through the morning's routine, her brief conversation with Brett played over in her mind.

She'd have to be careful. Brett wouldn't respond to her trying to make him feel guilty. She knew that instinctively. Just as he seemed to know too much about *her* instinctively.

If he saw through her so easily, he'd figure out what she intended before she'd even started. She couldn't let that happen.

Somehow Rebecca had to see to it he realized this was where he belonged.

Please, God. Please let this work.

Repeating her prayer silently, she went to see how Brett was doing with Minna.

"I don't believe it, that's all." Minna sat on the edge of the table, clutching the paper gown around her with both hands, a mix of anger and fear on her face. "You're just making a big mistake!"

The woman's words rang in Brett's ears. *You're making a big mistake.* Those had actually been the supervising physician's words when he found Brett following his ethics instead of the hospital rules. Brett had known in that instant that he would have to sacrifice his fellowship for his principles.

Now he was hearing those words again, and by the look on the woman's face, she didn't have much trust in her new doctor.

His jaw clenched. Whether she trusted him or not, he had to make her listen.

"Now, Minna, you don't mean that." Rebecca's calm voice cut through the tension in the small room. Just her presence seemed to take the level down miraculously.

"Dr. Brett is a fine doctor," she went on, "but if you'd rather see Dr. Overton, we can arrange that.

I'm afraid there will be a wait, though. He's so booked up today. It might delay your getting back to the shop.''

The woman's death grip on her gown relaxed a little. ''I can't have that.'' She scowled. ''What a mess that girl will make of things if I'm not there, and there are plenty of visitors in town today.''

Obviously Rebecca knew just what tack to take with the woman. Of course she knew the patients well. The Bedford Creek Clinic wasn't like a city hospital emergency room, where you treated someone and never saw him again.

''Now, Mrs. Dawson, I just want to run a simple test,'' he said. ''It'll take no time at all.'' He met Rebecca's gaze over the woman's head. ''EKG, okay?''

He saw the flicker of doubt in her eyes, and it nettled him. Who was the doctor here?

''Right away,'' she said, calmly professional whether she doubted his judgment or not.

''Don't see why I have to do that.'' Mrs. Dawson's lips pressed together. ''It's worse than usual, but it must be my indigestion, see? Doc always gives me a prescription, and that fixes me right up. I don't need any test.''

''This is like the one we did on your husband last year,'' Rebecca soothed. ''You remember. It's just a precaution.''

He seized on the word. ''Just a precaution. It'll only take a few minutes, and then you'll be out of here. And if you want, we'll have Dr. Overton take a look at the results, too.''

She nodded slowly. "Guess if Doc looks at it, it'll be all right.''

He suspected he knew what Rebecca was thinking. That he was being presumptuous, that he was overriding Doc's opinions. He nodded toward the hall, and Rebecca followed him out.

"You're thinking it's her heart?" Her golden-brown eyes were troubled.

He shrugged. "I don't like the pain she's having, or the rapid pulse." He tried a smile. "Could be because I was holding her hand, but I don't think so."

She didn't argue, but he could sense the reservation was still there.

"Well, we'll know soon enough."

He stayed out of the way while Rebecca went to get the EKG machine then returned to the exam room. The last thing the patient needed was any white-coat anxiety at the sight of a new doctor. Especially a new doctor she didn't particularly trust.

He frowned. He was more concerned about Doc's reaction. The first patient he saw, and she'd put him in the position of contradicting his old mentor. Doc had been treating her for indigestion, not angina.

He shook his head. At least Doc would probably be more forgiving than Dr. Barrett had been when Brett disagreed with him.

"The woman should have been sent to the county hospital." Dr. Barrett's tone had been icy. "They handle the indigent cases."

Brett could have protested that she needed care immediately, but Barrett would have disagreed. He could have said that for the first time in a long while he was doing what God called him to do, but that argument wouldn't have impressed Barrett. As far as Barrett was concerned, *he* was God in his little medical world, and no hapless resident should try to challenge him.

So Brett had put himself on the line, insisting the woman be admitted and going over Barrett's head when he had to. Barrett had given in, but the payback had come soon enough. The surgical fellowship he'd been a shoo-in for had disappeared.

"Here it is." Rebecca came out into the hall with the strip, just as Doc appeared. Obviously she had alerted him, and Brett felt another spurt of annoyance.

Doc reached for the strip. "Let's have a look."

His tone was neutral, but Brett's jaw tightened. He didn't like being in opposition to Doc, even though he was sure he was doing the only thing possible.

Doc frowned.

Brett's tension edged up. "How's it look?"

"The EKG is definitely out of normal range." Doc pushed his glasses into place on his nose, his hand fumbling with them. "I should have suspected it was more than indigestion before this. If I'd done an EKG last month, it might have shown something then.'' He handed Brett the strip. "Mind if I talk to her? It might come better from me. She'll have to go to the hospital for more tests on her heart.''

He shook his head. "Of course not. She's your patient. She'll want to hear it from you.''

He should feel good. He'd been right. But he couldn't erase the stricken look from Doc's eyes.

He stayed out of the way while Doc soothed the woman and talked to the husband called in from the waiting room, and Rebecca made efficient arrangements for her transport to the nearest hospital.

"Forty miles away.'' He stood next to her as she hung up the phone.

"Forty miles by mountain road.'' She grimaced. "It's okay for Minna, but sometimes...''

She let that thought trail off, but he knew what she meant. Forty miles might as well be four hundred, in some cases. Bedford Creek should have a better choice than one overworked doctor or a forty-mile drive.

"Now, you're going to be fine.'' Doc went to the door with Minna and her husband. "They'll take good care of you, and I'll be by to see you tonight.''

The fear seeped from the woman's face at the words. "All right, Doc. If you say so.'' She looked at him with absolute confidence.

The door closed behind them. Doc came back, rubbing his head wearily.

"You shouldn't drive clear over there tonight." The words were out before it occurred to Brett that Doc might take offense at his meddling.

Doc just shrugged. "Got to. She wouldn't rest easy if I didn't stop in. She trusts me." He straightened, looking at Brett. "That was a good call, Brett. I'm glad you were here today."

Funny. He'd forgotten, in all those years away, how much Doc's praise meant to him.

Chapter Three

Rebecca took a step back from Brett's smile, her heart thumping. He looked so... She wasn't sure what it was—but then suddenly she knew. He looked as if he belonged here once again, just as she'd hoped.

She tried not to jump to conclusions. It was a long way from treating one patient to deciding to stay. But she had to find out what he felt.

"I guess you get more exciting cases in Philadelphia, don't you?"

"Some." He shrugged. "But you're involved with people's whole lives here. That's worth a lot."

"It's satisfying."

So maybe Brett wasn't as happy in his big hospital career as he'd thought. Maybe, if she could talk him into helping at the clinic for a while, he'd realize this was where he belonged.

She eyed him cautiously as he consulted with Doc over a chart. He glanced up, gave her a quick smile and turned back to their consultation.

Her heart clenched. A quick smile—that's all it had been, but it had transported her back in time. She saw herself, an awkward thirteen-year-old, watching as the boy she loved pinned an orchid to her sister's prom gown. He'd looked up for an instant, noticed her and smiled. Then all his love and attention had veered back to Angela, leaving Rebecca alone and bereft.

She swallowed. "I'll order sandwiches from the café for lunch. Brett, what would you like?" She tried to sound like the cool professional she was.

He turned toward her, his arm brushing hers. Her breath caught in her throat.

If he stayed—as he must—they'd be working together every day. She had to find a way to handle that. She couldn't let Brett turn her into a lovesick adolescent again.

She wouldn't, that was all. He obviously still regarded her as his almost-kid sister. He'd never look at her any other way, and she didn't want him to. He wasn't the boy she'd fallen in love with, and she wasn't sure she even liked the man he'd become.

When lunch arrived from the Bluebird Café, they sat around the table in Doc's office with their sandwiches. Rebecca let the conversation flow between the two men, watching them. Doc was so tired, and yet so happy Brett was here. Didn't Brett see that?

Finally Doc pushed the empty sack away and stretched. "Good sandwich." He said that every day about the turkey club Cassie sent for him. "Do I have enough time to rest my eyes?"

She consulted her watch. "Plenty of time. You take a quick nap, and I'll call you five minutes before your first appointment."

"I don't nap," he said with dignity as he got up. "I just rest my eyes."

"Right." She smiled at Brett as the door closed behind him. "And he snores while he rests his eyes."

Brett smiled back, but then he sobered. "He's getting old. I know you said that, but I didn't believe it until I saw him. I always thought he'd go on forever."

"He thinks so, too." She tossed the lunch remains in the trash. "That's part of the problem. He won't take it easy. He can't. I'm afraid one day he'll lie down for his rest and not get up again." *Please understand.*

Brett frowned. "Is he all right? Has he had a thorough work-up?"

"As thorough as he'll let me do." She spread her hands flat on the table. This was the first time she'd felt able to talk to someone about this. If only she could tell him everything...but she couldn't. She'd promised Doc.

Still, it was good to share the worry. Good because it was Brett, whom Doc loved like a son and took pride in.

"He claims he's just tired out, that's all. He works a schedule that would exhaust a younger man, and he never takes a break."

Brett's green eyes darkened. "There has to be something we can do."

You can take over the practice, the way he planned. She closed her lips on that. It would only lead to another argument.

"Maybe he'd let you check him out." She hesitated, half afraid to say anything else. If Doc knew she'd suggested a checkup, he'd be furious. But she had to. No one else would. "Look, I know you said you were just here on a break." The word tasted bitter, but she pushed on. "But you could help out while you're here."

His frown deepened, creating three furrows between his eyes. "That's not a solution."

Her resolve slipped. "The best solution would be for you to stay."

He shoved back his chair, stalked to the window, and stared out at the aspen tree, tinged now with gold. "You really think that's what these people need? Horse-and-buggy medicine? A one-doctor town?"

She shot to her feet. "Doc's a good physician. He gives people everything he has."

He lifted his hand as if to stave off her attack. "I know that. But I also know it's worn him out."

She fought down her anger. Anger wouldn't help. She had to get him to make a commitment—just a small one.

"He needs a rest. He'd get that if you helped out for even a week before you go back to Philadelphia."

"I'm not going back to Philadelphia." He swung around, but she couldn't see his face clearly with the light behind him.

"What do you mean? Your residency—"

"I completed my residency. I thought I'd be starting a surgical fellowship, but the one I expected to have isn't going to be there."

His voice sounded flat, denying any emotion, but she knew better. She rose, moving toward him until she could see his expression clearly. It didn't tell her much. He was hiding something; she knew that without analyzing how or why she did.

"Then you're free to stay in Bedford Creek, aren't you?"

His mouth tightened at her persistence. "You'd better understand, Rebecca. I'm not prepared to settle down in this town for the rest of my life. There are other fellowships out there."

The anger she'd been trying to suppress spurted out. "So you're just home while you look for a new fellowship. You're going to ignore the debt you owe to Doc."

"I'm not ignoring anything." His green eyes sparked with anger. "This is between me and Doc."

"You haven't even told him yet!" She wanted to shake him. Didn't he understand what was at stake?

His face hardened, becoming the face of a stranger. "I'll tell him when we have supper together tonight. Until then, I'd suggest you stay out of it."

Brett found he was still fuming at the memory of that conversation as he drove up Main Street toward the café to meet Doc. Who did Rebecca think she was? She didn't have the right to interfere.

Didn't she? The reasonable question slid into his mind, deflating some of the righteous indignation he'd been fueling. She was obviously a big part of what kept the clinic going, so she had a stake in its future, if not in his.

Maybe part of his problem was the whole idea of little Rebecca, the tag-along kid sister, lecturing him about his responsibilities. A rueful smile touched his lips. He'd better admit it—he still hadn't gotten used to the grown-up Rebecca she'd become while his back was turned.

Who'd have guessed the gawky kid would blossom into a beautiful young woman? He'd found himself wanting to touch her cheek, just to see if it was as soft as it looked. Wanting to tangle his fingers in that silky hair...

Whoa, back off. This was little Rebecca he was thinking about—the Rebecca he'd always thought of as a kid sister. She undoubtedly still considered him a big brother. That was why she felt free to lecture him, just the way she would lecture Quinn. She'd never think of him any other way.

He couldn't possibly be attracted to her. He saw again those golden-brown eyes, warming with a smile for him, and felt a jolt that had nothing brotherly about it. Okay, maybe he could be attracted to her, but he wasn't going to do anything about it.

Nothing about a relationship with Rebecca could be at all casual, and he knew it, so there wasn't going to be anything. The future he had mapped out for himself didn't include the possibility of marriage for a long time. He travels fastest who travels alone—and he intended to keep moving.

So he'd ignore the surge of attraction he felt every time he saw Rebecca. Given the way she felt about him right now, that shouldn't be difficult. She'd be only too happy to ignore him.

He pulled into a parking space in front of the Bluebird Café, switched off the ignition and took a deep breath. Telling Rebecca he wasn't staying had been difficult enough. Telling Doc seemed almost impossible.

He got out and stood for a moment. The setting sun edged behind the mountain, sending streaks of orange along the horizon, softening slowly to purple. He'd forgotten how quickly twilight came in the narrow valley, closing in as the sun disappeared.

It had been a long time since he'd stood still and watched the sun go down. Peaceful. He could use some of that peace right now, as he prepared to break the news to Doc. He turned, pushed open the door, and saw Doc waiting at a table in the back.

The opportunity he needed didn't come immediately. Doc had already consulted the cardiologist who'd seen Minna at the hospital, and he clearly wanted to talk about his diagnosis and treatment plan. It wasn't until Doc had scooped the last bit of chicken gravy onto his roll and popped it in his mouth that he began to run out of shoptalk.

Finally Doc pushed his plate aside and propped his elbows on the red-and-white checked tablecloth. He peered at Brett over the top of the glasses that constantly slid down his nose, his faded blue eyes intent.

"Okay, out with it."

Brett discovered he was clutching the checked napkin like a lifeline. "What do you mean?"

Doc lifted his eyebrows. "You think I'm so old I can't tell when something's wrong with you?"

"No, I guess not." Some of his tension slipped away. "I've been working up my nerve to tell you something."

"Wouldn't have anything to do with a difference

of opinion you got into with a supervising physician, would it?''

He hoped his mouth wasn't hanging open. ''How did you know that?''

Doc shrugged. ''I still have my sources. You want to talk about it?''

The café was empty except for them, and Cassie James, the owner, after checking at least three times to be sure they had everything, had retired to the kitchen.

''There's not much to tell.'' Brett frowned, studying the bluebird on the heavy white coffee mug. He didn't want it to sound as if he were making excuses for himself. ''I was doing an ER rotation, and the paramedics brought in a street person in pretty bad shape. Standard procedure was to send them to county, but I felt she wouldn't stand the trip. I scheduled her for surgery.'' He took a breath, remembering. ''Dr. Barrett didn't agree, and I had to go over his head.''

''Were you right?''

He reached inside himself for the answer. Was he right? ''Yes.''

Doc nodded sharply. ''Then that's what matters. Forget Barrett. He's not as important as he thinks he is.''

''Unfortunately he's important enough to control who gets the surgical fellowship. And it's not going to be me.''

He met Doc's gaze, and saw instant sympathy

reflected there, followed by a sudden spark of hope. He had to get the rest of it out before Doc could build too much on his words.

"Doc, I know we used to say I'd come back here after my training and take over the clinic so you could retire." He found his throat closing. How could he say that the life Doc loved wasn't the one he wanted?

Doc looked away, seeming to stare out the window that overlooked Main Street. When he looked back at Brett, there was no condemnation in his face—just understanding. "Your dreams have changed."

He nodded. "Yes, I guess they have." His voice sounded husky, even to himself, and his throat felt tight. "I didn't realize then what possibilities there are in medicine. Now..."

"Now you want something more." Doc rearranged his cup and saucer, his hand trembling slightly. "Can't say I'm surprised. I guess I always figured you might discover talents you didn't know you had."

"I don't want to let you down." The strength of that feeling surprised him. "I'd never want to disappoint you. I'll repay every cent you loaned me. But I'd like to try for another surgical fellowship."

There, it was out.

Doc didn't say anything for a long moment. Then he smiled. "Any program head who doesn't take you is a fool.'' He reached out to clasp Brett's hand. ''You're going to make us all proud, son.''

''But you—''

''I'm not ready to retire yet,'' Doc said quickly. ''The right person will come along to take over the clinic long before I'm ready to hang it up. Shoot, what would I do if I quit? Chase a little white ball around a golf course? Not for me.''

''You might get to like it.''

''I like what I'm doing now just fine.'' Doc shoved his sleeve back to glance at his watch. ''Speaking of which, I'd better get on the road to the hospital. Minna's expecting to see me.''

''I'll pay you back, you know. I mean it.''

Doc shook his head. ''Help someone else instead.'' He put his hand on Brett's shoulder. ''It's all right, Brett. You're not letting me down.''

It was one thing to hear Doc say the words. It was quite another to believe them. Brett watched Doc make his way to the door, stop to exchange some joking words with Cassie, then go out. His shoulders were stooped, his walk almost a shuffle.

Pain gripped Brett's heart. It wasn't all right. Even if he didn't intend to settle down in Bedford Creek for the rest of his life, he couldn't just walk away. Somehow, he had to do something.

Rebecca sat on the front porch swing, watching the stars come out one by one in the sliver of sky that wasn't blocked by the maple trees lining the street. She should go in. She shivered, pulling her sweater more closely around her shoulders. Nights got cool in the mountains in September.

She glanced across the lawn to the house next door. She might as well admit it. She was waiting for Brett to come home from his meeting with Doc.

She'd really messed up her fine plan. She bit her lip. The plan wasn't at fault, her temper was. She'd let it get control of her tongue, and she'd antagonized Brett so thoroughly that now he'd never listen to her.

Lord, please help Doc do a better job of this than I did. I'm sorry I spoke hastily and messed things up.

The Lord must get tired of hearing her confess the same sin over and over again, she thought. She pushed the swing with her foot, listening to the comforting *creak.* Each time, she promised to try harder, but trying harder didn't seem to be the answer.

She tried to picture Doc and Brett talking together over their meal. She'd like to believe Doc was insisting Brett follow through on his promise. She'd like to, but she couldn't. Doc would never admit how desperately he needed help.

Headlights pierced the darkness, illuminating the trunks of the maples. Brett parked at the curb, got out, and stood for a moment, looking in her direction. Then he walked toward her, and suddenly her heart seemed to be beating way too fast.

Enough, she lectured. *Brett doesn't mean anything to you anymore, remember?*

His footsteps crunched through the fallen leaves on the walk. "Mind if I join you?"

She shrugged, moving over to make room on the swing. It creaked as he sat. He leaned back, and she tried to ignore the warmth that emanated from him. Tried, and failed.

"This has to be the same swing." He pushed gently with his foot. "I remember the creak."

"You should. You and Angela spent enough time out here."

She remembered, too. Remembered sitting at her bedroom window in the dark, listening to their soft, private laughter and the creak of the swing. Wishing *she* were sitting beside him.

"The good old days." He leaned back, staring up at the stars as she had done. "Seems like a lifetime ago."

"It probably seems longer to you because you've been so many different places since then." She bit back the words that wanted to spill out about where he'd been and where he was going in the future.

"I guess." He pushed again, the swing moving back and forth with a little more energy, as if it picked up on some agitation he didn't show.

She couldn't pretend she didn't know where he'd gone tonight, and she couldn't act as if it didn't matter. She'd just have to choose her words carefully, that was all. Brett seemed willing to forget their earlier quarrel, and she had no desire to remind him.

"Did you and Doc have a nice supper?" That was neutral enough, surely.

A faint smile flickered on his lips. "We ate at the Bluebird Café. Hasn't anyone in this town heard of healthy cuisine?"

"Only the newcomers. Let me guess. Doc had chicken and gravy."

He nodded. "Got it in one. And rolls with butter, and mashed potatoes."

"Nobody can resist Cassie's homemade rolls." This didn't seem to be getting them any closer to the subject she needed to discuss, but at least they weren't sniping at each other.

"Doc should at least cut down on the butter, and he knows it. That's what he'd tell a patient." He frowned, turning to face her. The swing stopped abruptly as he planted both feet on the porch. "He needs to retire."

"Did he say so?"

"No." He gave an exasperated sigh. "Of course he didn't say so." He shook his head. "Go on, ask. You know you want to."

He sounded frustrated, but not angry, so maybe it was safe to broach the sore subject.

"Did you tell him?" She held her breath, waiting for an explosion.

His jaw tightened. "Yes. I told him. I think he'd already guessed most of it."

"What did he say?"

"About what you'd expect."

She swallowed hard. "That's it, then." She hated saying the words. "He's given you his blessing. You can go away and forget about the clinic." *About us.*

"You know I can't."

She looked up at him. He was very close to her, but it was hard to make out his expression in the dark.

"What do you mean?" She held her breath. Maybe he was about to say—

"I mean you were right. I can't ignore this. I owe Doc too much for that."

Hope surged through her. "You'll stay?"

He shook his head, and the hope died as quickly as it had come. "I can't. Try and understand that, Rebecca. Doc does."

"I don't." If that was incitement to a quarrel, it would have to be. "You admit you owe Doc. Is that how you intend to repay him? By leaving?"

"I'll help out at the clinic for the time being." He sounded grimly determined. "And while I'm doing that I'll figure out a way Doc can retire with an easy mind. But as for the future..." He shrugged. "I don't think it's going to be the way you wanted."

She already knew that. Dreams didn't come true, not in real life. Prince Charming didn't come back for Cinderella.

"I guess not."

The swing creaked as he moved. Then he touched her chin lightly, the way he'd tease a smile from a child. The warmth of his hand flowed through her, and her heart stuttered.

"Don't think too badly of me, okay? Maybe none of us should be held to promises we make when we are kids. After all, you promised to marry me if I'd just wait until you were grown up."

He must feel the warmth that flooded her cheeks. "That was a long time ago."

"Now you're all grown up, and everything's changed." His hand still lingered against her cheek. "I've changed, too. But I'm going to do my best to help Doc, so I guess we'll be seeing a lot of each other."

A faint hope flickered. He'd be helping out at the clinic every day. Maybe being there would make him realize this was where he belonged. Maybe God was giving her another chance to convince him to stay.

The trouble was, she'd have to find a way to do it without having her heart broken by the man she'd given it to when she was five.

Chapter Four

The good thing about going to the café for breakfast, Brett decided, was that no one bothered you unless you wanted to talk. When he'd walked in the door, the early morning regulars had greeted him as if he'd been there yesterday morning, instead of years ago. Then they'd gone back to their newspapers or conversations about the weather and the state of tourism.

Nostalgia had prompted him into the third booth from the back, the one that had belonged to him, Alex and Mitch when they were in high school. The blue-padded seats looked like the same ones. With a mug of Cassie's coffee steaming in front of him, he shook out the newspaper and prepared to get up-to-date on Bedford Creek news.

Halfway through the front page, someone slid

onto the bench across from him. He looked up to find Mitch flagging Cassie and the coffeepot.

She got there before he could gesture again. "Like old times, the two of you sitting here together." She set the heavy white mug on the table and filled it in a swift, efficient movement. "You just need to get Alex here with you."

"We'll work on it." Mitch waved away a menu. "Just coffee, thanks."

Brett raised an eyebrow. "Does Anne have you on a diet?"

"I had breakfast two hours ago. Cops get an earlier start than doctors."

Mitch might have been up for hours, but his blue uniform was as sharply pressed as if it had just come off the rack. That was the lingering effect of years in the military, Brett had always supposed.

"When I was interning, I don't think I ever went to bed. Come on, Mitch, admit it. You've got it soft these days. Cushy job in a small town, beautiful wife-to-be..."

Mitch grinned. "Plus a couple thousand tourists, no staff to speak of and two kids."

"And you love it," Brett pointed out.

"And I love it." Mitch's smile softened, as if he were thinking of Anne. "I'm one lucky guy." Then his gaze focused on Brett. "What about you?"

The mixture of relief and guilt he'd felt the night before flooded back. "I told Doc last night."

"And?"

Brett shrugged. "Great, fine, I have his blessing. You know Doc. He wouldn't say anything else." Maybe that was what bothered him most—that Doc would be so unfailingly supportive, even when Brett was disappointing him.

"Look, you have to do what you're called to do." Mitch spread big hands flat on the table. That was what he'd said when Brett told him the day before. "We both know that. Doc knows it, too."

"I wish it were as clear-cut as that. If Doc were ten years younger, it might be. But I've seen him at the end of the kind of day he's putting in at the clinic. He's exhausted. It's time he took it easier— even thought about retirement."

Mitch shook his head. "Doc won't retire. Face it. He'd rather die in harness."

"I'm not going to let it come to that."

"So what are you going to do? You can't force him to take it easy. He's the only doctor in town, remember?"

The decision he'd made the night before still seemed right. "That just means I have to act fast. I have to find someone else to work at the clinic, eventually take over for him. That's the only way."

Mitch's skeptical look spoke volumes. "Easier said than done. The clinic board tried that a couple of years ago. The world isn't filled with doctors who want to settle down in a town of five thousand, miles from anywhere. And anyone who was interested, Doc didn't think was good enough."

"There has to be someone." Stubborn determination filled him. "And I'm going to find him. Or her. I've already talked to Rebecca about it."

Mitch frowned. "I guess we both know what Rebecca thinks you should do."

"She's made that abundantly clear," Brett said. His mouth twisted wryly. "She looked about ready to have me horsewhipped when I said I wasn't back to stay."

"I can imagine. She feels pretty strongly about Doc."

"I know." Brett turned the bluebird-patterned mug in slow circles on the tabletop. "I don't quite know why she's here, though. She could have gone anywhere when she finished her training."

"That's about when her father was diagnosed with cancer," Mitch said. "You know how close they were. Rebecca came home to see him, and just stayed. Doc was in and out of the house all the time. John Forrester was a friend as well as a patient."

"He was a good man." John Forrester—quiet, unassuming, honest—had been part of Brett's life for as long as he could remember. "I can understand why she came back then, but not why she stayed."

"I guess she felt her mother needed her," Mitch said. "Face it, Angela's got a good heart, but she doesn't have a whole lot of common sense. And when Quinn's wife died, his little girl moved in with them. Rebecca's got her hands full, I'd say."

"Yes, I guess she has." And probably a big debt she felt she owed Doc.

"One thing's sure." Mitch smiled, but his eyes were serious. "If Rebecca thinks anything you do will hurt Doc, she really will horsewhip you. I guarantee it."

Rebecca couldn't let it go. She paused in the parking lot outside the clinic, lifting her face to the September sunshine. That conversation with Brett ran through her mind over and over again.

He would leave. That was the bottom line. He'd try to solve Doc's problems before then, but she knew the reality of the situation, even if he didn't. He wouldn't find a solution—not in a few short weeks, not even in a few months, probably.

That panicked sense of time running out gripped her again. What was she going to do?

She closed her eyes. *Help me, Father. Please. You'll have to guide me, because I don't know what to do.*

When she opened her eyes, the autumn colors seemed a little more golden. She took a deep breath, some of the tension in her shoulders ebbing. Now if she could just remember to leave the burden in God's hands, instead of picking it up again, she'd be better off. She took another deep breath and walked into the clinic.

Brett was already there. He stood at the cabinet, looking over some files, and her heart thudded at the sight of him. He glanced up, sea-green eyes frowning, and waved a chart at her.

"Where are Alex's medical records?"

She frowned right back. "Are you seeing him today?"

"No." He eased away from the drawer, looking surprised that she'd question him. "But I'd still like to see them."

She hesitated. What would Doc say to that? Brett didn't really have any official standing, but...

"You're the one who wanted me here," he reminded her, seeming to finish the thought for her. "If I'm practicing medicine and treating Doc's patients, I have a right to see the records."

And he expected her to jump to do his bidding. She stiffened. It was easy to forget that kind of attitude existed when you worked for Doc, who always asked, never ordered.

"Yes, Doctor," she said with careful formality. She marched to the cabinet and pulled the files he wanted. "The records are on the computer, as well."

He reached out, but instead of taking the folder he closed his hand over hers. Her pulse ricocheted against his grip.

"Sorry." He gave her a rueful smile. "I didn't mean to snap. I was preoccupied. Thank you." He released her hand, took the files.

She had to resist the urge to put her fingers over the warm spot where his touch had been.

"You're welcome." Her gaze met his and lingered. Then she cleared her throat and stepped back, heart pounding. "Is Doc in yet?"

"I'm here."

She spun at the sound of his voice. Doc stood inside the back door, eyeing them with an expression she couldn't interpret. She felt her cheeks grow warm. How long had he been watching?

"Brett." Doc walked toward them and dropped his bag on the countertop. "I didn't expect to see you today."

Brett shrugged. "I thought you might be able to use a little help while I'm in Bedford Creek. You're not going to kick me out, are you?"

"Course not." Doc's gravelly voice roughened a little. He turned toward his office, then looked back over his shoulder. "Rebecca, will you come in when you have a minute?"

She followed him into the office. Once the door was closed he looked at her, frowning a little. "Why is Brett here?"

She felt instantly guilty, as if Doc had heard her discussing him with Brett. "I...well, you heard him. He wants to help out while he's home."

"You suggest that to him?"

She couldn't lie to Doc, of all people. "I told him I thought you ought to take it easy for a bit. But coming in today is his idea. He wants to be here."

Doc's frown deepened. "You didn't tell him about my little problem."

"That series of dizzy spells you're having isn't a 'little' problem."

"Two isn't a series. Did you tell him?"

If only she could believe there had just been two. "No, of course not. But I think you should."

"Out of the question."

"But, Doc, he cares about you."

"That's why," he said gruffly. "Bad enough having you hovering over me, telling me to rest, wanting me to see a specialist. I don't want to hear it from him, too."

"I haven't given you advice you wouldn't give any other patient." Her mind raced through the possibilities suggested by Doc's dizzy spells, his forgetfulness. None of them was good.

"I'm fine." He dodged that truth, as she knew he would. "If Brett wants to help out, all right. But I'm holding you to your promise. He's not to know."

"He won't hear it from me."

But if Brett was the physician Doc thought he was, he'd figure it out for himself, sooner or later. What would his reaction be? Apprehension prickled her skin. She might have predicted the reaction of the idealistic young Brett he used to be. But not of the man he was now. And she wasn't sure she could trust what he might do with the knowledge.

* * *

The day's routine started to roll, carrying her with it and wiping out the time for worrying. Rebecca quickly discovered that handling the system for two physicians was considerably more difficult than handling it for one. By afternoon she sensed that she, like Doc, was falling behind.

She was on the phone, trying to set up a series of tests Doc had ordered, when Brett appeared in the hallway and dropped a chart in front of her.

"I've finished with the maternity case. Did you do the preliminaries on the next patient?"

She put her hand over the receiver. The lab had put her on hold, anyway. "Not yet. I'm setting up some tests for Doc." And how could he possibly be done with his last patient already?

"Can't someone else do that?" He frowned, looking around the office as if expecting to see a complete staff suddenly appear.

"There isn't anyone else, except the receptionist. And she doesn't have a firm enough touch to deal with the lab. They'd be scheduling Doc's patients for the middle of next year if she did it."

His fingers drummed on the countertop. "This isn't a good use of your time or mine."

Her temper flared. "You've been here less than twenty-four hours. Do you think you know your way around the clinic better than—" The lab came back on the line just then, interrupting her before she could say anything more. "No, that won't do," she said firmly. "Tomorrow at the latest." The lab prepared to argue.

Brett, frowning, picked up the next chart and went to call the patient himself. The expression on his face annoyed her so much that she snapped at the lab, with the surprising result that Doc's patient was scheduled for that very afternoon.

She hung up, feeling guilty. She shouldn't have snapped, either at Brett or the lab.

My temper, again, Lord. I'm sorry.

Brett was relentlessly formal the rest of the day. By the late afternoon lull, she knew she had to do something to make amends. She fixed a mug of coffee and carried it into the office, where Brett was catching up on some of the endless paperwork.

At least, that's what she'd thought he was doing. She found him on the phone.

"...must know someone." He paused at the sight of her, then gestured her in. "Sure, that's okay. It's a town-owned clinic—currently one doctor and a physician's assistant."

He reached for the mug. She was so stunned that it took her a moment to react. She handed it to him.

"Tell anyone who's interested to contact me here. Thanks a million, Tom. I won't forget it."

He hung up.

"You're already looking for someone else."

He turned a surprised look on her. "Of course. Isn't that the whole point?"

"I just didn't think you'd be working on it already."

"You mean you hoped I wouldn't be working on it at all."

Maybe that was what she'd hoped, but she didn't intend to admit it to him. "You're not wasting any time."

The words came out more bitterly than she thought they would. She'd known he'd do this, but she hadn't expected it so quickly. She'd thought he'd take the time to get used to the clinic's needs, involving himself while he did. She'd thought she'd have more time to convince him to stay.

Brett pushed himself away from the desk, standing to lean on it with both fists. "That's right. I said I didn't intend to let Doc struggle on his own, and I don't. If I can get a couple of viable candidates, I'll present them to the board."

"Doc will have something to say about whether they're viable or not."

"Let me handle Doc." He seemed to withdraw, becoming again the stranger she didn't know. "Just don't interfere, Rebecca. I'm doing what's best for all of us."

She bit back the words that would lead to an open breach between them. She couldn't afford that, not when there was the slightest chance he'd decide to stay. He might think he could talk Doc into something else, but she knew better. But her hope was becoming dimmer by the moment.

* * *

Rebecca walked into the house with a sense of relief. Home. The welcoming atmosphere surrounded her as soon as she closed the door. She could relax and give herself a brief respite from worrying about Doc or thinking about the clinic. Best of all, she could stop fretting about Brett Elliot.

"Aunt Rebecca!" A small tornado hurtled down the steps. Kristie threw herself at Rebecca, trusting she'd be caught.

"Hi, sweetie." Rebecca hugged her, enjoying the feel of small arms around her neck and silky hair against her cheek. "How was school today?"

"Come see." Kristie tugged her toward the living room. "See all my papers." She pointed to the array spread atop the coffee table.

The kindergarten class had obviously been painting. Bright colors splashed across large sheets of construction paper and ran exuberantly into each other.

"Wow. Did you do all those?"

Kristie nodded proudly. "I wore my painting shirt, and I didn't get any paint on me. See?" She stretched out her knit top for inspection.

"That's great, Kristie." She leaned over the table, hoping she'd be able to recognize something. "What a lot of nice colors you used."

"See, there's Grandma's house." Kristie put a small forefinger on a gray blob.

With that lead, Rebecca was able to identify the rest of the picture. "You painted the tree house. Neat."

"And there's Daddy." Kristie's voice wavered a little on that, and Rebecca's heart cramped.

"Who's this?" She pointed to two stick-like figures under a tree.

"That's me and Jeffy on the playground."

This was something new. "Are you and Jeffy getting along better now?"

She nodded. "I told him what Dr. Brett said about my hair. Dr. Brett knows lots more than Jeffy does, doesn't he?"

"I guess so." And why she should be so annoyed at having to admit that, she didn't know. She was glad Kristie had resolved her differences with Jeffy, even if Brett had been the catalyst.

"I like Dr. Brett." Kristie leaned against her confidingly. "Don't you, Aunt Rebecca?"

"Sure she does." Angela stood in the archway, looking at Rebecca with a mischievous smile.

"Angela..."

Her sister ignored the warning note. "She's always liked Dr. Brett. A lot."

"I was five at the time," Rebecca said shortly. "I grew out of it."

"I don't think so." Angela scooped Kristie up and danced with her across the room. "When Brett took me to the prom, you were green with envy— admit it."

Her cheeks got ridiculously hot. "I won't admit any such thing. When are you going to grow up? You're the one who was madly in love with Brett, remember?"

Kristie's eyes got huge. "Are you in love with Dr. Brett, Aunt Angela?"

"Course not, silly. I'm in love with Ron. We're going to get married, and you're going to be the prettiest flower girl there ever was."

"But Aunt Rebecca said—"

"She was just teasing, sweetie." She set her niece down. "You scoot into the kitchen. Grandma wants your help with supper."

Kristie darted through the swinging door to the kitchen.

Rebecca frowned. "I wish you wouldn't say things like that in front of Kristie. What if she repeats it?"

Angela's blue eyes sparkled with mischief. "So what? And that's a great idea, don't you think?"

"What's a great idea?"

"You. Brett."

"What about me and Brett?"

"You've always been crazy about him."

"Stop saying that." Rebecca glared at her. "It's not true."

Angela's eyebrows arched in disbelief. "He's back. You're here. You have a lot in common. Maybe this is your chance to get together with him."

"Get together? Angela, that is the most ridiculous thing I've ever heard."

"Why? It's not like you're seeing anybody else. Neither is he, as far as I can tell. I think you'd be great together."

"I think you're overdosed on wedding plans. Brett doesn't see me that way, and I am certainly not interested in him."

"I don't know. I saw the way he looked at you at the party. He couldn't take his eyes off you."

Her heart gave a silly little *thump*. "That's just because he expected me to look like a kid."

"You could—"

"Forget it!" Rebecca glared at her. "No matchmaking, understand? Just because you're engaged doesn't mean you can go around putting everyone else in pairs."

The doorbell rang, cutting off whatever retort Angela might have made. Rebecca went quickly toward the welcome interruption, pausing for one last word over her shoulder to her sister. "And I absolutely do not want to hear another thing about Brett Elliot."

She yanked the door open. Brett stood on the porch.

After a frozen moment, he raised his eyebrows. "Am I too early?"

It was an echo of the first conversation they'd had when he came back. "Too early?"

"For supper."

When she didn't answer, a smile quirked his lips. "Let me guess. You didn't know your mother invited me for supper tonight. And you're not delighted at the news."

Chapter Five

Brett had been pleasantly surprised at the call from Mrs. Forrester inviting him to supper. Judging by the expression on Rebecca's face, she was equally surprised, but not pleasantly.

Maybe she'd just have to get used to the idea. Mrs. F had always had a soft spot for him, and he'd like her to go on thinking well of him. This dinner invitation was his chance to... What? Justify? Explain? That suddenly seemed kind of petty.

Rebecca, apparently becoming aware that she was blocking the door, stepped back with what should have been a welcoming gesture.

"I'm sorry. Mom didn't mention it to me. I was just surprised."

Soft peach color bloomed on her cheeks, reminding him again of the longing to touch. That feeling was better ignored.

"Maybe she thought you'd object if she told you." He moved inside, unable to resist the urge to tease her, just a little.

Her color deepened. "Of course not. After all, it's not as if it's the first meal you've had here."

"I did mooch quite a bit back in the old days, didn't I?" When he and Angela dated, and even earlier when he and Quinn had played ball together, he'd probably had as many meals here as at home.

"You were always welcome."

Rebecca's stiff reply amused him, but before he could tease her again, a small figure bounded into the hallway, closely followed by Angela.

"Dr. Brett!"

"Hi, Kristie. How's everything? Anyone called you carrottop lately?"

"I told Jeffy what you said," she announced. "So he doesn't call me carrottop anymore." She held out her hand. "Want to see my pictures?"

Angela linked her arm through his, smiling at him. "Let him relax, Kristie. He doesn't want to look at pictures now."

He didn't need the sharp glance from Rebecca to tell him what to say to that. He freed himself and took Kristie's hand. "Sure, I'd love to see them. What about Aunt Rebecca? Did she see them yet?"

Kristie nodded. "She said they're really colorful." She turned to Rebecca. "But you can look at them again, Aunt Rebecca, if you want to."

"I need to change my clothes first." Rebecca

edged toward the staircase. "You show Brett, all right? Especially the nice one with you and Jeffy."

Since he didn't think Rebecca was anxious to get away from her niece, he suspected he was the cause of her sudden need to disappear. He smiled at her. "I'll see you at supper."

She nodded, then turned and hurried up the steps.

With a proprietary air that amused him, Kristie led him to the living room and proudly displayed her artwork. He made admiring noises, conscious that he was relaxing in an atmosphere that didn't seem to have changed in the last fourteen years. The same comfortable, overstuffed chairs, what looked like the same framed photos on the piano... Mrs. F must find reassurance in the familiar.

He could feel Angela growing impatient next to him as Kristie's art show continued. When the little girl pulled out the papers she proudly called her homework, Angela shook her head.

"Not now, Kristie. Brett and I want to visit. You go help Grandma in the kitchen."

Kristie pouted. "But I have to do my homework. Somebody has to help me."

"You know Aunt Rebecca will help you later. She always does. Go on, now, scoot."

So Aunt Rebecca was the one who helped Kristie with her homework, as well as tucking her into bed and painting the tree house with her. Rebecca seemed to be taking on most of the parenting duties with her brother's child.

He'd expected to enjoy catching up with Angela. But after listening to endless details about Angela's engagement, her wedding plans and her fiancé Ron's apparently brilliant career at the bank, he found he longed for Rebecca's return. Even when Rebecca was arguing with him, she was never boring.

But Rebecca didn't reappear until they gathered around the oval dining table. There her mother seemed to take it for granted that Rebecca would ask the blessing and supervise Kristie's meal.

Mrs. F handed him the platter of pot roast. "I fixed your favorite, Brett. You see, I haven't forgotten how you boys used to eat."

If he ate like this on a regular basis, he'd be a walking blimp. "Looks wonderful." He forked off the leanest piece he could see, and found Rebecca watching him with suppressed amusement in her amber eyes. She obviously knew just what he was thinking. "It's too bad Quinn can't be here to enjoy it."

"Poor Quinn." Mrs. F's soft brown eyes filled with quick tears. "You know about his loss."

"He knows." Rebecca sent a warning look toward Kristie.

Again he was surprised by the sense Rebecca was the responsible one. Why should Rebecca, the baby of the family, be the one who took charge? Because she wanted to? Or because no one else would?

It occurred to him that John Forrester, for all his quiet, unassuming air, had been the glue to hold the family together. Apparently Rebecca had taken over where her father had left off.

Angela handed him a steaming bowl of mashed potatoes. "Brett, we're just dying to hear about your plans. I know they're lots more exciting than anything we're doing in Bedford Creek."

"Oh, I don't know. Things seem pretty…controversial around here to me."

He watched Rebecca flush again at his use of the word. They both knew most of the controversy was between the two of them.

Rebecca's smile had an edge to it. "Do tell us about your plans. We all want to hear."

His gaze clashed with hers. He wasn't about to let little Rebecca make him uncomfortable, so he responded with a brief résumé of his completed residency.

Rebecca lifted her eyebrows. "And what comes next?" Her unspoken criticism came through loud and clear.

"I hope to do a surgical fellowship next. I have a couple of applications out, so I'll see where that leads."

"Where would you go?" Angela seemed more interested in the locale than the position.

"One's in San Francisco, one's in Chicago." He shrugged. "It's just wait and see, right now. Wish me luck."

If he'd been hoping for encouragement and support, he got it from Angela and her mother. But in the midst of their enthusiasm, he found he was watching Rebecca. Funny, suddenly her opinion was the one that mattered.

And he already knew what that opinion was.

Rebecca clenched her water glass until her fingers whitened. Why on earth had her mother invited Brett tonight of all nights? Things were happening too fast. She hadn't yet had an opportunity to process everything that had been said between them during the day, and now here he was, sitting across the table from her, perfectly at ease.

Or was he? She watched his strong fingers grip his knife as he cut the meat deftly. Maybe he was holding on a bit too tightly, just as she was. Maybe this evening wasn't any easier for him than it was for her. Oddly enough, the idea made her feel a bit better.

She turned to encourage Kristie to eat her peas, then snatched another quick look at Brett. His tanned skin glowed against the forest-green shirt he wore, echoing the green of his eyes. The strong line of his jaw, perhaps a little tense, accented the cleft in his chin. Fine lines crinkled around his eyes as he responded to some laughing remark of Angela's, and her heart suddenly hurt.

She'd felt this way before—the awkward, tongue-tied little sister—watching the two of them laughing together. They'd always seemed charmed, as if nothing could dent their perfect lives.

She gave herself a mental shake. Brett and Angela weren't a couple anymore. They'd broken up their senior year over Brett's determination to go away to college. And she wasn't a kid. She had to stop slipping back into childish ways of looking at Brett Elliot, and figure out how to deal with him.

"…why, I almost thought he didn't remember that I'd been in just the week before with bronchitis."

Her mother's voice penetrated her thoughts, and she realized with alarm that they were talking about Doc. How long had that been going on, while she'd sat there mooning about Brett?

"I suppose he'd just been busy. After all, he sees a lot of patients in the course of a week," Brett said. But he sent her a questioning glance, and her tension level cranked upward.

"Well, I know Rebecca mentioned that he—"

"More potatoes, Brett?" Rebecca thrust the bowl toward him, interrupting whatever heedless words her mother was about to utter. Not that she could blame Mom. She shouldn't have voiced her worries about Doc—not to anyone.

"No, thanks." The words were casual, but his sharp glance wasn't.

"Rebecca, you can see we're finished. Why don't you clear while I bring in the dessert and coffee." Her mother turned to Brett, distracted for the moment from the subject of Doc. "I made apple crumb pie, just for you."

He'd better have a big piece and eat every crumb, or Mom's feelings would be hurt, she thought as she headed for the kitchen. But she didn't need to worry about that. Brett always managed to say the right things. Maybe that was why he'd gone through school in his perfect charmed circle, while she'd stumbled around, saying the wrong things and then being embarrassed and regretful.

She rinsed the dishes and stacked them quickly in the sink, then hurried back. What indiscreet things might her family say if she weren't there to head them off?

"Hasn't the clinic board done anything to help Doc out?" Brett was saying when she returned. "After all, running the clinic is their responsibility."

He gestured with his fork, as if pointing it toward the five-member board charged by the town to oversee the clinic. Her heart clenched. This was dangerous territory.

Angela shrugged. "You know they've never had to work very hard at that job. They always just take Doc's word for everything. I don't think they even checked Rebecca's references when they hired her on his say-so."

"My references were perfectly fine." Rebecca reminded herself not to get distracted from the real point. "The board does their best. They're devoted to Doc."

"I'm sure they are." Brett frowned.

Was he thinking the board should be devoted to the welfare of the town, not to Doc? Brett's words about horse-and-buggy medicine rang in her mind.

Her mother broke in with a comment about the difficulty of getting good people to serve on the town's boards, and the conversation became more general. But Rebecca couldn't relax, her mind twisting and turning with a new worry.

The clinic board was devoted to Doc, yes. But how might they react if they knew he wasn't well? They'd want, as she wanted, the best for him. Would they see the quandary, as she did?

How could you do the right thing for Doc if he didn't want it? How could you do it without hurting him terribly in the process?

By the time her mother pushed her chair back from the table, Rebecca could feel only relief that this interminable meal was over. Kristie slipped from her seat and darted around the table to clasp Brett's hand.

"You wanted to see my tree house," she reminded him. "Let's go now, okay? Aunt Rebecca, will you come with us? Please?"

She picked up the dessert plates. "You go ahead. It's my turn to wash the dishes." The excuse would do as well as any to get her out of Brett's disturbing presence for a little while.

Angela snatched the plates from her hands. "It's not your turn, it's mine."

Rebecca looked at her sister blankly. "No, it's not." This sounded ridiculously like the arguments they'd had as kids. But it wasn't Angela's turn, it was hers. And Angela never took an extra turn— not unless forced into it.

"Yes, it is." Angela nudged her. "Go on, Brett's waiting. You and Kristie show him the tree house."

Angela's blue eyes sparkled with mischief, and Rebecca suddenly realized what was going on. That teasing earlier had had a point. Angela was match-making, with her and Brett, of all people.

"Go on, dear," her mother prompted. "Brett is waiting."

She was outmaneuvered. If she went on arguing, it would only call attention to the fact that she didn't want to be in Brett's company.

She managed a smile and a nod as she took Kristie's hand. It looked as if she'd end up back in that tree house with Brett, whether she wanted to or not.

Now what, exactly, was bothering Rebecca about showing him the tree house? It had been perfectly clear to Brett that something unspoken was going on between the Forrester sisters in that little exchange. But what?

He followed Rebecca and Kristie through the kitchen and out the back door, into the tree-shaded yard. Again, he had the sense that nothing had changed.

"Still looks the same. I see your mother's thumb is as green as ever." A vegetable garden flourished in a sunny spot. Pumpkins, beginning to shade from green to gold, sprawled among still-laden tomato plants.

Rebecca smiled, some of the tension seeming to go out of her. "She grows enough to feed the whole neighborhood. People run and hide when they see her coming during zucchini season."

"The lilacs are higher." He nodded toward the hedge that separated the Forrester backyard from his parents'. "I used to be able to see over it."

"You mean you used to spy over it on Angela and her girlfriends, don't you?" Teasing him, Rebecca became the friend of his childhood instead of an adversary he had to battle. "Of course, they'd have been disappointed if you hadn't."

"I remember." It seemed an eternity ago, and yet in some ways as fresh as yesterday. "Where would you have been? Hiding in the tree house so you could listen to them?"

"Probably," she admitted, her smile reluctant. "I was always trying to figure out the secret."

Kristie ran to the tree and swarmed up the ladder.

"Secret?" He stepped under the trailing branches of the weeping willow, holding them back for Rebecca. She stepped inside. He let them fall, and the leafy green barrier enclosed them in a private world.

"You know. The secret. What made them so popular." Rebecca's nose wrinkled, as if she still tried to figure it out. "I wanted to be like them, but I guess I always knew I never would be."

His heart caught at the image of the child she'd been, hiding in the tree house, wishing she were the beautiful, popular older sister. "Then you grew up and had your turn."

She shook her head, laughing a little. "Trust me, I never caught up with Angela in the popularity department." She gestured toward the ladder nailed to the trunk. "After you."

He grabbed a rung and shook it. "You sure this thing will hold me?"

"If it doesn't, there's expert medical attention right at hand."

Above him, Kristie peered over the edge of the platform, wiry red hair falling around her face. "Come up, Dr. Brett. I won't let you get hurt."

"I'll hold you to that, Kristie." Aware of Rebecca watching him, he started to climb.

Actually, the ladder was perfectly solid. He should have known Rebecca would make sure of that before she'd let her little niece play in the tree house. *Responsibility* seemed to be Rebecca's middle name.

He reached out a hand to Rebecca as she scrambled up after him, suddenly longing to understand what made her the person she was. That was logical enough, he told himself. If he understood her better, maybe he'd see a way to get her on his side.

He clasped her hand, pulling her up, and as she scrambled over the edge she leaned against him for an instant. Her warmth and softness sent a jolt right through him, and he knew perfectly well that he had more than one reason for wanting to understand Rebecca Forrester.

Kristie gave him an escorted tour of the tree house, complicated by the fact that it really wasn't large enough for three.

The second time Rebecca brushed against him, she abruptly sat down, her back against the trunk. "Maybe I'd just better stay in one place. After all, I've seen the tree house."

"Is the tire swing new?" Brett asked. "I don't remember it."

Kristie nodded, her curls bouncing. "Aunt Rebecca put it up, just for me."

Of course it would be Rebecca who'd done it. "It's great. Doesn't it make you dizzy, though?"

She shook her head violently. "I can spin and spin and not get dizzy. I'll show you."

Before he could stop her, she scrambled back down the ladder and hopped on the swing. He turned, groaning a little, and sat down beside Rebecca. "Where does she get that energy? After that meal, I just want a nice nap."

Rebecca's smile was tinged with sadness. "I

didn't realize how much she misses her daddy until I saw how she reacted to you. I think she's just showing off for you.''

"How is Quinn?" He lowered his voice so Kristie couldn't hear from the swing. ''I'm sorry I mentioned his name at the table. I didn't mean to start anything awkward.''

"It wasn't your fault. We need to be able to talk naturally about Quinn in front of Kristie, without bringing up Julie's death.''

"I was so sorry to hear about it.'' He didn't want to imagine how Quinn felt, losing his wife, in an instant, to a drunk driver.

She nodded. "It's pretty difficult and lonely for him. We're trying to do our best with Kristie, and he talks to her every day.''

He studied her serious, intent face. "Don't you mean *you* are?"

Her golden-brown eyes met his, startled. ''Well, we all are.''

"Yes, but mostly Aunt Rebecca. You're supposed to be the baby of the family, remember? Who made you the responsible one?''

He said it teasingly, but in the sudden darkening of her eyes he saw that he'd hit a nerve. He clasped her hand in an instinctive gesture. "I'm sorry, Rebecca. What did I say?''

She shook her head, but not before he'd caught the sheen of tears in her eyes. "Nothing. It's all right.''

"It's not nothing." He lifted her hand, holding it warmly between both of his. "Something upset you. Come on, if you can't tell an old friend, who can you tell? This tree house has seen plenty of secrets in its time."

He felt her hold out against him for another moment, then the need to talk seemed to overcome the need to keep her secret.

"It's just…that's what my father said to me. About being the responsible one. He said every family has someone who's the responsible one, and it's not always the one people think it should be."

It didn't take a genius to read between the lines. "When he was ill, you mean."

"When he was dying," she corrected softly. "I was working in Boston when he got sick, and he wouldn't let Mom tell me or Angela how serious it was. Finally Doc called and broke it to me. I came home right away so I could take care of him."

Remembered pain tightened her face, making her look older than her years. He longed to take the pain away, but that was another one of the things he couldn't do.

"You were here when he needed you most. That's what counts."

"I hope so." She shook her head. "Sometimes I think I should have seen something earlier. If I had been here, maybe—"

"Don't." He gripped her hand more tightly. "People always think that, and medical personnel are the worst about it. You know Doc did everything that could possibly be done.''

She nodded. "I know." She gave him a watery smile that almost broke his heart. "In my mind I know, but in my heart—" She broke off, then started again. "How we'd have gotten along without Doc I can't imagine. He and Pastor Richie were here every day toward the end. Doc sat up with Dad at night so I could get some sleep. Mom and Angela tried, but they got too upset.''

He felt as if something had a stranglehold on his heart. "Doc's that kind of person. He's always there for you."

"Yes." Her gaze met his, forthright and honest. "I owe him everything."

They both knew what she was saying. He'd wanted to understand what made her tick, and now he did. Rebecca had every reason in the world to protect Doc, and no reason at all to see things Brett's way.

Chapter Six

"Let us pray."

Rebecca bowed her head obediently as Simon Richie began the pastoral prayer, but her mind persisted in straying to her own concerns.

She yanked her wandering thoughts back to the prayers of the church. *Lord, why can't I stop worrying about this situation and leave it in your hands?*

Next to her, Kristie wiggled, then settled when Angela frowned at her. Rebecca handed her the crayons she'd put in her bag as she did every Sunday, and Kristie began coloring the bulletin.

The past few days at the clinic had left her increasingly unsettled. It had been bad enough to be constantly in Brett's company before the night he'd come to dinner. It was worse afterward.

Each time she was near him, she relived those moments in the tree house when they'd been so close. She'd confided in him the way she had at five, when her worst worry had been learning to ride a two-wheeler.

At least, it had seemed that way, right up until the moment he took her hand in both of his. The resulting tingle had moved from her hand straight to her heart. Now, each time she was with him, she seemed to feel that again.

Her discomfort would be worth it if her plan was working, but she didn't see any sign of that happening. Brett showed up at the clinic every day promptly, he saw patients, he consulted with Doc. In Doc's eyes, it was probably just as he'd dreamed it would be. And he must be hoping it wouldn't end, even though he knew it would.

But Rebecca knew about the calls Brett made to what seemed a wide network of medical acquaintances, putting out feelers for a replacement. Next he'd probably be putting ads in the journals.

Well, no, he wouldn't do that without talking to the clinic board. But that could be next on his agenda, and she didn't know what to do.

Please show me, Lord. I don't know what else I can do to get him to stay.

She tried to concentrate on the rest of the service. And when she couldn't, when her restless mind refused to cooperate, she focused on the Emmaus window behind the pulpit. Morning sunlight streamed through it, illuminating the figures of Jesus and the two disciples on the Emmaus road that first Easter. It had never failed to comfort her in the past, and it didn't fail now.

She lingered for a few minutes after the benediction instead of following her family, listening to Ellie Wayne play the postlude on the organ. Ellie's long, dark hair fell like a curtain hiding her face, but the arc of her body over the keyboard expressed the devotion that flowed through her fingers.

Somehow the sight, the music, and the light streaming through the window combined to bring the peace that had eluded her for days. She got up, breathing a silent prayer of thanks. God would give her the answer in His own time, not hers.

She emerged from the sanctuary to find the hospitality committee serving lemonade on the lawn. People clustered around white-draped tables laden with platters of cookies and fruit. She could see a number of tourists mingling with the regulars.

She was helping herself to a cup of lemonade when Anne Morden came up beside her. "Have one of the oatmeal squares," Anne said. "Emilie thinks they're wonderful." She bounced the toddler on her hip, and Emilie waved a sticky cookie at Rebecca.

"You keep that one, sweetheart. I'll get one of my own." Rebecca blew a kiss to Anne's adopted daughter.

"Did you try on your dress yet?" Anne smiled and shook her head. "Listen to me. I sound like every other bride-to-be, totally preoccupied with my wedding. I'm sorry, Rebecca. How are things going at the clinic?''

"Yes, I tried on the dress." The simple street-length dresses Anne had chosen for her attendants suited Rebecca. "The alterations will be done next week. And things are fine at the clinic."

She thought she'd sounded perfectly normal, but Anne shot her an inquiring look. Maybe, being an attorney, Anne had learned to listen to what lay behind the words.

"What's going on? I thought Brett was helping out."

"He is." She followed Anne's glance across the lawn, to where Brett stood with Alex and Mitch—who were talking about football, to judge from the gestures. Davey, Mitch's foster son, hung on every word.

"Then what's wrong? I know you've been worried about Doc's workload." Anne grasped her daughter's hand just before the sticky cookie landed on her dress.

"Here, let me." Rebecca took the baby wipe and mopped Emilie's hands and face, to be rewarded with a smile. Emilie had to be one of the happiest babies she'd ever seen.

Anne put her daughter on the grass, then turned her determined look on Rebecca. "Don't evade the subject. Isn't it helpful to have Brett there?"

"Yes, of course. It's just…" She couldn't tell

Anne the worst of it—the battle that was going on in her heart every time she was near him. "It just makes me realize how bad it will be when he leaves."

"Maybe he'll stay." Anne watched her husband-to-be laugh at something Brett said. "I mean, look at the three of them together. Their friendship really means a lot to them. Maybe Brett will realize he'd be happier here, with people who care about him."

Anne's words dropped into Rebecca's mind and settled. Why hadn't that occurred to her, in all her struggling? Anne was right. Brett's lasting friendship with Alex and Mitch could be a strong motive for staying in Bedford Creek, if he'd let it.

Was there a way she could remind him of how much that friendship meant to him? She looked at Anne, wondering.

"Are you and Mitch going to the festival kickoff on Wednesday?" The Fall Foliage Festival was a four-day extravaganza designed to lure tourist dollars, but it generally ended up being even more fun for the townspeople.

"I gather it's not something we can miss," Anne said. "Mitch has been complaining all week about the extra work it causes the police department, but I think he's looking forward to it."

"Maybe Brett would like to join you." She hoped the suggestion didn't seem pushy. "I mean, since his parents aren't around."

Anne gave her a speculative look. "That sounds like a good idea."

"What sounds like a good idea?" Mitch appeared at Anne's side. Alex and Brett were right behind him.

Rebecca's heart gave that familiar, annoying little lurch at the sight of Brett. She ought to be getting used to it by now.

Brett knelt and held out his hands to Emilie. "How's my pretty girl? Come see Uncle Brett."

Emilie launched herself into his arms, and he stood up, smiling.

"We were just talking about the Fall Festival kickoff," Anne said.

Mitch groaned. "Don't remind me. I've been recruiting every available volunteer to direct traffic." Even in a suit instead of his uniform, Mitch looked every inch the police chief he was. "It's a massive headache."

"You love it," Alex said. His dark, often somber face creased in a smile. "Admit it. You wouldn't miss it for anything." He turned to Brett. "You are coming Wednesday night, aren't you?"

"Why don't you join us?" Anne said quickly. "Both of you, and your little boy, of course, Alex. It'll be fun. Rebecca's coming, too."

Faces turned toward her, and she had to hide her consternation. That wasn't what she'd intended when she'd mentioned inviting Brett to the festival.

Brett looked at her, arching an eyebrow. "Are

you, Rebecca? You'd better. I need protection from all these kids.'' He bounced Emilie, and she squealed.

Rebecca pasted a smile on her face. An evening in Brett's company was a small price to pay if it helped convince him Bedford Creek was where he belonged.

''Of course. I wouldn't miss it.''

Rebecca had managed to get through most of Monday morning at the clinic without being alone with Brett. She'd consider that a major accomplishment, except that it didn't seem to be solving the problem of her reaction to him. She didn't need to be alone with him to feel a wave of warmth every time his gaze drifted to her, or to flush whenever he smiled at her.

Professional—that was the attitude she had to maintain. She straightened her lab coat, running her hand over the bronze nameplate. She had to stay professional in her dealings with him, in spite of her mother asking him to dinner, in spite of Angela's matchmaking, in spite of the prospect of spending Wednesday evening in his company. Her heart gave a little *thump* at the thought. And that was another thing that had to stop.

Militantly erect, she marched into the office where he'd holed up after seeing his last patient of the morning. She'd find out what he wanted for lunch, and she wouldn't let herself be distracted by the cleft in his chin or the way his eyes crinkled when he smiled.

Brett looked up from the computer. "Lunchtime already?"

"Just about." She couldn't help glancing at the screen to see if he were perusing the physician-wanted ads. But the display seemed to be an article from a medical journal. "Doing some research?"

"In a way." He swung the screen to face her. "Take a look at this."

She leaned across the desk to read it, uncomfortably aware of the spicy scent of his aftershave. The piece seemed to be a report on a new technique in complex knee surgery.

She glanced at him, finding his face very close to hers, his eyes intent. She straightened, breathing a little quickly. "You're thinking this technique might be a solution for Alex?"

He frowned. "I don't know. I certainly don't want to second-guess Doc, but I'd like to see Alex making more progress than he is."

His affection for Alex came through clearly in his voice.

"I know." The words came out impulsively. She didn't want to second-guess Doc, either, but he would always put the patient first. "You know Doc would welcome any suggestions. Why don't you take this to him?"

"There's not enough here." He looked frustrated. "This cross-references another article, but I can't get it to come up." He gave her a half smile. "Maybe the machine is just out to get me."

"Let me give it a try." She leaned across again, trying to ignore his nearness. "There are a couple other ways it might be listed."

He tossed his pen onto the desk. "If I'd started my surgical fellowship by now, I'd be in a lot better shape to give advice."

Rebecca clicked, frowned, and started another search. "You never did tell me what happened." She shot a questioning glance at him, realizing she might be treading too close to a painful subject. "I'm sorry. If you don't want…"

He leaned back in the desk chair. "It's nothing that complicated, although I have to say it seemed pretty traumatic to me at the time." He shook his head. "I was working the ER when paramedics brought in a street person. Standard procedure was to send them to the county hospital, but I was afraid she'd lose her leg if we did that. So I sent her up to surgery. The chief of service didn't approve."

She wasn't fooled by his dry tone. "It must have been a bad scene."

His mouth twisted. "The worst. I'd dared to defy him, and even went over his head to get her admitted. That was something he didn't take from any resident. He didn't file any charges against me, but the next day I found out the surgical fellowship I had counted on had evaporated. I guess I'd known that from the look on his face, anyway."

"Why did you do it?" He might not answer, but she really wanted to know. She'd have guessed he was too intent on his career to make waves with someone who had that kind of power.

He shrugged. "Because I trusted my judgment. Because…" He frowned. "For the first time in a long while I really felt God was calling me to do this." He glanced up at her. "Dr. Barrett would have thought that deluded, at best."

"I wouldn't," she said softly. Her heart clenched. She hadn't had to make any difficult faith choices like that. She only hoped that if she did, she'd be strong enough to do the right thing.

His green gaze met hers—met and held. The moment stretched out, motionless in time. She felt as if she were seeing all the way to his soul in those emerald depths. Her breath caught.

Brett shook his head suddenly, glancing away from her, breaking the bond. "What—" He cleared his throat and nodded toward the computer. "Are you finding anything?"

That was it, then. He didn't want to share that kind of moment with her. Well, she didn't either, did she? Where had her resolution to stay professional gone?

"I don't think so. Wait, yes, here it is. Do you want me to print it out?"

"Print out a couple of copies, so you can go over it, too. I'd like your opinion."

That didn't mean anything, she told herself. He

just wanted her professional opinion, nothing else. And that was good, because that was all she had to give him.

She handed him the first copy off the printer, then took the second one for herself. She leaned against the desk and tried to concentrate on the article.

When she looked up, Brett's green eyes were shining. "What do you think? On paper, Alex sounds like a good candidate for the surgery, don't you think?"

She saw the enthusiasm in his face. "Maybe. But there might be things we don't know about it, things that would eliminate him from consideration."

"At least we have something." He grabbed her hands in both of his and squeezed them. "You don't know how much it means to me to find something that might help. Thank you, Rebecca."

Any notion she'd had that she was in control of her feelings vanished with the warmth that flooded through her at his grasp. "I...I'm glad I could help." She realized she was stammering and took a deep breath. "I know your friendship means a lot to you. Maybe, a few months from now, you'll be able to see Alex throw his cane away for good."

A shutter seemed to come down over those clear green eyes. "Maybe." He muttered the word, and she knew in an instant what he was thinking. He was thinking that in a few months, he wouldn't be in Bedford Creek to see anything.

Brett was still thinking of Rebecca as he drove home that evening. He wondered if her reluctance to attend the festival with him stemmed from their continuing disagreement over the clinic. They were as far apart as ever on that subject. Or was it that she felt the same surge of attraction he did and was determined to deny it?

He pulled into the driveway. The bed of chrysanthemums by the garage was putting on a brilliant display of bronze, in spite of being ignored. He probably ought to spend some time on yardwork while he was here.

And thinking of things he ought to do, he really ought to forget the feelings Rebecca stirred in him. It would be far better for both of them if he could go on treating her like a little sister. Because the bottom line was that eventually he'd be leaving, so anything between them could only lead to disappointment.

He'd reached the porch when he heard a step behind him on the walk. He turned.

"Dr. Elliot?" The man—middle-aged, middle height, middle everything—had the indefinable air of someone who didn't belong in Bedford Creek.

"I'm Brett Elliot. What can I do for you?"

"Matthew Arends." He held out his hand. "I'm an administrator at Lincoln Medical Center."

Brett did a quick mental review of the cases he'd seen in the last few days as he shook hands. None of them, other than Minna, had been sent the forty miles to the large regional hospital.

"What can I do for you, Mr. Arends? If this is about one of our clinic patients, you really should talk to Dr. Overton."

"No, it's nothing like that." Matthew Arends looked rather pointedly toward the house. "Mind if we go inside to talk?"

Brett shrugged, then opened the door and led the way into the living room.

Arends glanced around as he took the armchair Brett indicated. "Lovely room. This is your parents' home, I understand?"

Now how and why did Arends have that information about him? Brett nodded. "I'm in Bedford Creek briefly. What is this about?"

"You prefer to come to the point, I see." Arends leaned forward. "Excellent. So do I. This is about the Bedford Creek clinic. Or rather, it's about the future of the clinic."

Brett hoped his expression didn't change. "Again, any questions about the clinic should be directed to the doctor in charge. I'm just helping out for a few weeks."

Arends's face remained expressionless. "We've had several discussions over the years with Dr. Overton about the clinic. Right now, what we'd like to do is enlist your aid."

Dealing with bureaucrats was a skill he'd never really mastered. "My aid to do what? Exactly what do you want?"

"We're prepared to make the Bedford Creek clinic a part of Lincoln Medical Center's satellite clinic network. Prepared, that is, if we can come to a reasonable agreement."

Brett hoped he didn't look as dumbfounded as he felt. What on earth was going on? If the regional hospital actually wanted to take over the clinic, why hadn't Doc mentioned it to him? And why was Rebecca so worried about what the future held?

"I can see you're surprised." Arends folded his hands neatly. "But it's not such an unusual development. You might even call it the wave of the future in medicine. These small one-doctor clinics are a thing of the past."

"Horse-and-buggy medicine." The words were out before Brett had a chance to think about it.

"Exactly." Arends beamed. "I can see we think alike about this subject."

Brett shook his head. "You're still talking to the wrong person. Dr. Overton is in charge of the clinic."

"As I mentioned, we've talked to Dr. Overton a number of times. He doesn't seem interested in our offer, and the clinic board has always been guided by his wishes. Of course, he's nearly retirement age. The question arises as to what will happen to the clinic when he's no longer able to carry on."

"And you'd like to take over." He suppressed a wave of optimism. On the surface it sounded like the perfect solution for everyone, but there were bound to be drawbacks. "Frankly, Mr. Arends, I'm surprised. I wouldn't think the practice here in Bedford Creek would be large enough to interest you."

"Well, the clinic wouldn't stay in Bedford Creek, of course," Arends said, as if it were a given. "That wouldn't be practicable. We'd combine the Bedford Creek clinic with the one in Townsend."

That had to be the main reason Doc wasn't interested in the center's proposal. He wouldn't want his patients to drive nearly twenty miles every time they needed to see a doctor.

"I still don't see what you want from me."

"Your influence," Arends said promptly. "From what we understand, you're the one person who might persuade Dr. Overton that this is best for everyone. I'm sure you see the advantages."

"I suppose." It was the kind of medicine he was used to—the big hospital, with its expensive technology and its ranks of specialists, staffing the small local clinic. "Much as I appreciate what your facility has to offer, I don't know that I feel comfortable trying to influence Dr. Overton if he's not interested."

"Well, now, we both know how reluctant these elderly physicians can be to accept changes." Arends rose. "Just let me send you some information on what we have to offer. You can look it over and make a decision. That's all I ask."

Brett got up slowly. "I can't make any promises."

"Fair enough." Arends held out his hand. "We aren't asking for anything more than that you consider it."

Consider it. Brett stood at the doorway and watched Arends drive away. He'd be hard put to think of anything else, now that the man had dropped a possible solution to everyone's problems right in his lap. Not just everyone—Rebecca. If this went through, Rebecca would be free to leave Bedford Creek. He didn't want to picture a future in which he wouldn't be seeing her.

Chapter Seven

"Doc?" Rebecca rushed across the examining room the next morning. Doc leaned against the table, hand to his head. "What is it? What's wrong?"

He straightened instantly. "Nothing. I'm fine." But his face was pale, his eyes tired.

"Don't fib to me. I can see you don't feel well." Her fingers sought his pulse.

"Just tired."

"I'm getting Brett." Ignoring his objections, she hurried to the door.

Doc was firmly in control of himself by the time she got Brett to the room. He allowed Brett to do a quick exam, insisting the whole time he was fine.

Brett's gaze met hers over Doc's head, and he shrugged. "You're taking the day off, Doc. Like it or not. Rebecca and I won't take no for an answer."

"That's right," she echoed.

Doc glared at them for a long moment. At least she had Brett to share the intensity of that look. She wouldn't have been able to stand up to it alone.

Finally Doc nodded. "All right. Just today, mind."

She could breathe again. "I'll drive you home." Doc would have walked the four blocks as always, but she wouldn't let him walk home.

When she got back to the clinic, after leaving Doc in his housekeeper's capable hands, Brett was dealing with an office full of patients. He greeted her with a lifted eyebrow as he grabbed a chart.

"Everything okay?"

"As okay as possible, I guess."

The urge to pour out her worries about Doc's health nearly overpowered her, but she'd promised Doc. She wouldn't break her word—not un-less...well, not unless it was a life or death situation, she supposed.

It wasn't, not yet—but at some point it might be. She was stuck between two bitter alternatives, and there didn't seem any way out.

Brett, apparently taking her words at face value, went on to the next patient. Giving herself a mental shake, she took the patient log from the reception-ist. Dealing with the day's problems was all she could do. At least Brett was there to share the load. For the moment, anyway.

At some point in the hectic rush, she realized that

one of the patients Brett had finished with hadn't yet come out of the exam room. Frowning, she glanced at the chart. Wanda Peterson, pregnant with her first child. She tapped on the door, then opened it.

"Wanda? Do you need some help?"

Wanda slumped in the chair, tears welling over. Rebecca knelt beside her.

"Wanda, why are you crying? Are you in pain?"

"N-no." She rubbed her eyes with the back of her hand. "I'm okay."

Rebecca pulled the other chair close, taking both of Wanda's hands in hers. "You're not okay, or you wouldn't be crying." She gave a regretful thought to whatever patients were still waiting. Some delays couldn't be helped. "Tell me about it."

"I guess I'm being silly." Her lips trembled. "But Dr. Brett said it wouldn't be long now, and I started thinking about how I never did this before, and what if it hurts as much as people say, and what if something's wrong with the baby..." She ran out of steam and choked back a sob.

"Did you say any of this to Dr. Brett?"

Wanda shook her head. "I was going to ask him, but he seemed like he was in such a hurry, I didn't want to bother him. And now I'm bothering you." The tears threatened to overflow again. "I'm sorry."

"It's not a bother," Rebecca said firmly. She put her arm around the young woman's shoulders, mentally reading the riot act to Brett. Why hadn't he seen how apprehensive the patient was? "I'm sure the baby's as fine as can be. You haven't noticed any difference in his activity, have you? Or in the way you feel?"

"No. Except that some days I really want to go and get it over with, and other days I don't want it ever to happen." Wanda's face screwed up with anxiety. "Is something wrong with me?"

"You're just like every other woman who ever had a first baby," Rebecca assured her. "Everyone feels that way."

"They do?" Sunlight began to break through Wanda's tears.

"They do."

It took another five minutes of reassurance, but when Wanda left the office she was smiling. Rebecca held her smile until the woman was out of sight, and then stormed off to find Brett.

Luckily he was alone, making notes on a chart. He looked up when she pushed through the door, eyebrows raised.

"Something wrong?"

"You bet something's wrong." She tossed Wanda's file at him. "You just saw Wanda Peterson."

"The maternity case. So? She's fine."

"She's not a case." She said the words distinctly. "She's a twenty-two-year-old having her first baby, with no family in town for support. She's not fine. She's scared. And you certainly didn't help any."

His face tightened. "She didn't say anything to me about being frightened. If she had—"

"She didn't say anything because you were in too much of a hurry. She didn't want to bother you."

"I'm not a mind reader, Rebecca." Anger flashed in his green eyes. "And I don't need you to tell me how to handle patients."

"No, you know how to handle them, don't you?" She was too angry to think of being tactful. "Is that what they taught you at the big city hospitals? Treat your patients like numbers and get through with them as quickly as possible? That's not how Doc runs this clinic."

He strode toward the door. "Doc's not here, remember? You're the one who wanted me to stay. So don't complain now that you've gotten what you wanted."

If the swinging door could have slammed, he'd probably have slammed it. As it was, he gave it such a push that it swung wildly back and forth for several minutes.

She'd lost her temper again. She'd said too much, and already regretted it. Oh, not that she'd spoken up. She'd had to do that. She didn't regret the content, just the way she'd delivered it.

Brett had changed. The idealistic boy she'd known had vanished, and he was probably gone for good.

Brett wasn't done fuming yet when the receptionist announced Alex Caine was there to see him. The reverence in her voice suggested that special treatment was due the local aristocrat who happened to be the richest man in town.

Brett managed a smile at her attitude. He'd known Alex too long to be awed by the Caine name. Alex was just his friend, a friend he wanted badly to help.

Pushing away his irritation with Rebecca, he rose to shake hands as Alex came in. It must be one of Alex's bad days, since the cane he sometimes used was in evidence.

"Doc says he'd like you to have a talk with me." Alex's intelligent dark eyes said he knew who to blame for that. "What's up? Some new medicine for which you'd like a guinea pig?"

"Not exactly." Brett spread his hands flat atop the file on the desk. "You know I wouldn't experiment on you, don't you?"

Alex cocked an eyebrow. "What about when you fixed me up with that cousin of yours? If that wasn't an experiment, I don't know what was."

"Amanda?" He grinned, relaxing. "Actually she turned out pretty well. But back in high school…"

"You told me she was a cheerleader at her

school. You didn't mention it was an all-girls school and she was captain of the basketball team and five eleven.''

Brett shook his head. ''You shouldn't let yourself be so influenced by a girl's looks.''

''I was fifteen,'' Alex reminded him. ''I was just as dumb as most fifteen-year-old boys. You owe me, pal.''

The casual words pierced Brett's heart. He did owe Alex, although not in that way. Maybe this was finally his chance to repay him.

''How's this for evening things up?'' He made an effort to keep the words light. ''I think I can help you get rid of that cane for good. And the pain that goes with it.''

Alex's expression didn't change, but something flickered briefly in his dark eyes. ''I'm listening.''

He'd given a lot of thought to how he'd present this to Alex. He didn't want to give the impression this was in any way a sure thing. The surgical technique was new, but it had worked in a number of difficult cases.

Brett watched Alex's face as he worked his way through what Brett had to say. He leveled with Alex, giving him a careful presentation of the technique, the pros and cons, the successes the surgeons had experienced.

He might not give all the details to some patients, but he knew Alex would demand to know everything. He knew, too, that Alex was intelligent enough to understand.

You see, Rebecca, he addressed her silently, *I have a perfectly good manner with patients, even if it's not exactly like Doc's.*

But Rebecca wasn't there to argue with him. He felt a faint twinge as he tried to concentrate on Alex's questions. Maybe Rebecca had a point, but she'd managed to hit a sore spot with her criticism.

He took back the article he'd given Alex to read. "So, any more questions?" He tried to keep his voice casual. He didn't want to pressure Alex. He might need more time to see the advantages to the surgery.

"No, you've made it perfectly clear." Alex frowned down at the cane. "I appreciate the time and study you've put into this, Brett."

He hadn't expected Alex to jump up and down with excitement, but he had anticipated more enthusiasm than that. "This could be the answer for you."

Alex nodded slowly. "I can see the advantages you describe. But it's not for me."

He couldn't be hearing correctly. He'd expected some hesitancy, but not a flat turndown. "I don't think you understand. This could get rid of your pain entirely if it works."

"If it works," Alex repeated, then smiled slightly. "I understand what you're saying, Brett. You're looking at possibilities. But I have to look at what's right for me—for my family and my business. I'm afraid this isn't it."

He stood before Brett could marshal an argument. "Thanks, pal. I appreciate it." He held out his hand. "See you at the festival, right?"

All Brett could do was nod. "Maybe we could talk about this more later."

"I don't think so." Alex limped toward the door. "But thanks."

Brett stared at the closed door for a long moment. Didn't Alex understand what Brett was offering him? He wanted to go after Alex, make him listen, but it seemed fairly clear that doing so wouldn't help.

He'd just hit the downside of a medical practice back in the old hometown. It hurt too much when you couldn't help someone you cared about.

He'd probably felt more useless than this sometime in his life, but he couldn't think when. Maybe he'd been in Bedford Creek too long. Maybe it was time he got back to the kind of impersonal medicine he was really cut out to do.

He thought again about Arends's proposal for the clinic. If it worked, it could solve everyone's problems. He ought to sound Doc out about it, but first he had to be better prepared.

The information Arends had sent painted a rosy picture. He needed to know the downsides and try to find solutions to them before he could hope to convince Doc that this was the answer.

The photo album was on the bookshelf next to the piano. Rebecca pulled it out that evening and sat down on the piano bench. She leafed slowly through the pages, not sure what she was looking for.

There were tons of pictures of Quinn, the oldest. Her parents had used up plenty of film on him. Quinn and Brett playing basketball in the driveway, Quinn and Brett in their peewee baseball uniforms.

And Angela, of course. Angela in her dancing class tutu, Angela in her scout uniform, Angela with the flute she'd attempted to play. And finally, Angela with Brett when they started dating.

She bit her lip. Was this what she was looking for—this boy with the smile that would charm the birds from the trees? This was the Brett she remembered—kind, handsome, patient with the obnoxious kid she'd no doubt been. This was the boy who'd told her he was going to be a doctor and come back to Bedford Creek and take care of all of them.

He'd changed in so many ways she couldn't begin to count them. He was certainly still handsome; that hadn't changed. His face, green eyes lit with laughter, formed in her mind, and her heart seemed to skip a beat. Actually that *had* changed. He was far more dangerously devastating now than he'd been at sixteen.

Was he still kind? Maybe, when he took the time to be, but unfortunately he didn't seem to be taking that time. And all that lovely idealism had vanished as if it had never been. The only glimpse she'd seen of it had been when he'd talked about why he risked his fellowship by defying the senior physician.

He'd said he was doing what he felt God called him to do. She frowned down at the photo album.

Aren't You calling him to stay here and honor his promise, Lord? And if You are, why isn't he listening?

She closed the book on all those bright, innocent young faces. Maybe she was being naive to think promises made then meant anything now. Life changed people.

Certainly her brother had never anticipated the grief that was in store for him. And Angela, who'd talked for years about when she'd be old enough to leave Bedford Creek for the big city, was settling down perfectly happily in her hometown.

Brett had changed, too. That was what Rebecca had to remember. In one sense, maybe, that change was just as well. It certainly ought to make it easier for her to ignore the feelings she had for him.

She shoved the album back on the shelf and glanced at the mantel clock. Nearly seven-thirty. Time to round Kristie up and get her ready for bed.

Her niece didn't seem to be in the house. Rebecca glanced out the front window, then went to the back door. Kristie was probably out on the swing. That had become a favorite spot lately.

She glanced around the yard, rubbing her arms

in the evening chill. No Kristie. She had opened her mouth to call when she heard the voice above her.

Kristie was in the tree house again. And she wasn't alone. That was the rumble of a masculine voice answering her. *Brett.*

She walked closer, reluctant to call and disturb what seemed to be a serious conversation. Just outside the veil of willow branches, she paused.

"...wish my daddy was here." Kristie's voice was soft and sad, like the coo of the mourning dove that came to the bird feeder.

"I bet you do. I'd like to see him, too. We were friends a long time ago, when we were about your age."

"Did you know my mommy?"

Rebecca's breath caught. That was the first time Kristie had voluntarily spoken of her mother since Julie's death. Rebecca was conscious of an edge of resentment. Kristie's confiding should have been in her, not Brett.

"No, I'm sorry I never met her." Brett was gently matter-of-fact, probably not wanting to overreact. "I've seen her picture, though. She was very beautiful."

The night was so still that Rebecca could hear Kristie sigh. "I wish I could be beautiful like her. But Grandma says I look just like my daddy did when I was his age."

"You know what? I think your Grandma's wrong about that. You look a lot like that picture of your mommy. And I bet when you grow up you'll be just as beautiful. And you know what else? I'd say every time your daddy looks at you, you remind him of her.''

"You think so?" Kristie sounded as if she wanted to believe him, but couldn't quite manage it.

"I do. I really, really do."

That was the confident Brett charm that had convinced Rebecca of far more improbable things when she was Kristie's age. Tears stung her eyes. She could only hope it convinced her niece, too. She brushed the dangling branches aside and reached the ladder.

"Hey, up there."

Brett leaned over the edge. "Come on up."

If he didn't remember the bitter words with which they'd parted earlier, she did. "I think it's time for Kristie to get ready for bed."

Kristie's small face appeared next to Brett. "Just a little bit longer, Aunt Rebecca," she wheedled. "Please."

"Please, Aunt Rebecca," Brett echoed. He smiled down at her, his earlier anger apparently forgotten, or at least put aside for the moment.

"Just for a little bit," she agreed.

She climbed the ladder, pretending she didn't see the hand Brett held out to help her. But as she reached the top, he grasped her arm, pulling her over the edge with apparently effortless strength.

She landed between him and Kristie, a little breathless.

It would be too much to hope he didn't notice.

He raised an eyebrow. "Getting out of shape, Aunt Rebecca?"

She started to deny it heatedly, then realized that would raise the uncomfortable question of why, then, she was out of breath. She settled for a smile and put her arm around Kristie.

"Aren't you getting chilly, honey?"

Kristie shook her head, snuggling closer. "I'm warm enough."

On Rebecca's other side, Brett seemed to radiate heat. She tried to keep from touching him, but that wasn't easy in the confines of the tree house.

She glanced at him, lifting her eyebrows. "Giving some good advice?" she said softly.

He shrugged, looking at Kristie with a tenderness she hadn't seen in his eyes for a while. "Just listening, mostly."

"Tree houses are good for confidences." She stroked Kristie's wiry red hair. With a gentle sigh, Kristie leaned over, pillowing her head in Rebecca's lap.

"Yes, they are." Brett brushed her arm as he reached across to pat Kristie.

Warmth tingled along her skin.

He'd changed from his slacks, dress shirt and lab coat to jeans and a flannel shirt, the sleeves rolled back to the elbows. She tried not to think how ruggedly handsome he looked that way.

"Thank you." She murmured the words, trusting that Kristie, already half asleep, wouldn't understand what she meant.

Brett's smile was gentle. "Any time. I seem to remember a few conversations with you up here."

She nodded. She should be glad he seemed willing to forget their quarrel, but the unexpected intimacy of the moment disturbed her. An owl called somewhere in the woods; something, a cat or a rabbit, perhaps, rustled in the lilac hedge. Otherwise, they seem to be alone in the quiet universe.

Brett glanced up through the overhanging branches. "Look, the first star." He pointed toward a pinprick of light. "Remember we used to call out when we saw the first star."

"And first to see the streetlights come on," she added, smiling at the memory. "Kids still do that. I've heard them on summer nights, playing hide-and-seek in the hedges."

He leaned a little closer, so close that the scent of him touched her. "I'm glad that didn't change... glad some things are the same here."

"Kids still play the same games we did." She stroked Kristie's hair gently. "With the addition of some computer ones, of course. People still go to church, raise their kids, join the PTA. Bedford Creek doesn't change all that much."

"Really is like Brigadoon." His words gently

teased, reminding her of their conversation that first night.

"It's good to have a place where you can rely on things." She hoped she didn't sound defensive. "And people." She shivered a little, thinking suddenly of Doc. None of them would be able to rely on Doc much longer. He'd seemed fine when she'd checked on him this afternoon, but she knew the truth.

"You're cold." He put his arm around her, tugging her and Kristie close to his side.

She felt the soft nap of his flannel shirt, the warm smoothness of his skin. She tried not to lean against him, but she couldn't seem to help herself. "Brett—" She looked up at him, not sure what she wanted to say.

The moonlight filtered through the branches of the willow tree, touching his face. It made his hair look almost silver and cast shadows along the strong line of his jaw. Her breath caught, and words vanished.

Brett went very still, his gaze intent and searching on her face. He was so close that she could feel his breath against her cheek.

"No." She pulled back from him, heart pounding. "I mean, it's getting late. Kristie's almost asleep. I'd better get her inside."

He held her for another moment, then eased away, nodding. "I'll climb down first, and you can hand her to me."

His voice sounded perfectly natural, as if he hadn't been affected at all by that moment of closeness. She couldn't say the same for herself.

Her conviction that the changes in him made it easier for her to ignore her feelings seemed laughable now. There was no possibility at all of ignoring the way Brett made her feel, no matter what he did.

Chapter Eight

"Aren't you ready yet, Aunt Rebecca?" Kristie popped into Rebecca's bedroom with the question for the fourth or fifth time.

Rebecca smiled at Kristie's reflection in the mirror. "Just about."

"That's what you said the last time." Her niece bounced with excitement. "Dr. Brett just came out his front door. You have to be ready."

Her pulse insisted on racing at that bit of news. "You go talk to him," she said. "I'll be right down."

Kristie vanished, and her footsteps thumped down the stairs. Rebecca stared at herself in the glass.

It was ridiculous to be taking this much trouble over what she wore to the festival. Everyone would be in jeans, anyway. Nobody would be interested in whether her turtleneck matched her eyes, or whether she took the navy sweatshirt or the green windbreaker for later. And nobody would notice how her cheeks flushed at the thought of a whole evening in Brett's company.

At least, she hoped nobody would. She snatched up the green jacket, smoothed the patchwork quilt that had covered her four-poster since she was three and hurried toward the stairs.

In the hall below she heard Brett's deep voice, saying something laughingly to Kristie. The teasing note seemed to touch something deep inside her, something she couldn't shrug off.

Well, she'd have to hide it, that was all. Thank goodness they'd decided to take Kristie to the festival; thank goodness they'd be with a group of people. She could only hope that would keep her from betraying her silly susceptibility to Brett Elliot. She took a deep breath and started down the stairs.

Seen from above with the hall light shining on him, Brett's hair lightened from gold to flax. She wasn't going to notice how broad his shoulders looked in the forest-green sweater. She wasn't—

He looked up and saw her. His clear-as-glass green eyes darkened. He smiled slowly, the lines around his eyes crinkling in the way that made her heart turn over.

She gripped the railing, then forced herself to return his smile and walk steadily down to meet him.

"Rebecca." Brett looked from her to Kristie. "I don't know how I got so lucky. I get to escort the two prettiest girls there tonight."

"Aunt Rebecca's not a girl," Kristie protested. "She's a grown-up woman."

"I noticed." Brett's gaze lingered on Rebecca's face long enough to raise a flush. "Believe me, I noticed." He reached out to adjust the collar of her turtleneck. "Matches your eyes," he said softly.

She had to put a stop to the way Brett's touch made her feel. "We'd better get going. We don't want to keep the others waiting." And she certainly didn't want to be alone with Brett with only Kristie as a buffer between them.

The secret amusement in Brett's eyes suggested he knew just what she was thinking. He took Kristie's hand and gestured toward the door.

"Ladies, your carriage awaits."

The festival centered on the park that ran beside the river at the valley floor. Brett wove carefully through the crowds of people who meandered, apparently confident no one would hit them, across the narrow street. He backed expertly into the last available spot.

"I'm glad to see this is still a park." He held the door as Rebecca slid out. "Nobody's tried to put up condos or pave it for extra tourist parking."

Rebecca helped Kristie put on her jacket. It was already a little chilly so close to the river. "You've forgotten the flooding we get sometimes. Nobody's foolish enough to want to build in the flood plain, even if the town would let them.''

She glanced across the smooth green swath that stretched from the railroad tracks to the water. It was crowded now with booths and people, and lights winked in the gathering dusk.

''Nice, isn't it?'' Brett's voice softened as he followed the direction of her gaze. ''I'm glad we decided to come.'' His hand closed over hers, and her pulse beat so fast that she was sure he must be able to feel it.

She saw Mitch beckoning them. ''Look, there they are.'' Relief flooded her as they started across the lawn to join the others.

Mitch and Anne had toddler Emilie in a stroller, while Alex's son, Jason, trailed along with Davey. Alex had apparently left his cane behind for the evening, but Rebecca easily read the pain lines in his face.

What had happened between Brett and Alex when Alex came to the clinic? Brett had been terse and irritable the rest of the day, suggesting things hadn't gone as well as he'd hoped. She thought she saw some reservation now in the greetings he and Brett exchanged.

A moment later she told herself she'd been imagining things, as the three men began swapping stories, each one beginning *Remember when...*

She and Anne exchanged amused glances, then

fell into step with each other. This was what she'd hoped for from this evening. So why did she feel abandoned?

They wandered easily through the park, stopping each time one of the kids wanted to try a game or buy a hot dog.

"Let me get that." Brett's hand closed over hers as she reached for her bag when Kristie stopped at the candy apple stand. "She's going to break the bank tonight."

"It's for a good cause." It took an effort to ignore the warmth of his grip. "Everything raised is going toward the new fire truck for the volunteer firemen. We ought to be nearly there by the end of the week."

He smiled, lifting one finger toward the boy behind the counter. "Are we milking the tourist dollars to pay for the truck?"

"The festival did start out that way. But I think we enjoy it more than the tourists."

He handed the sticky candy apple to Kristie and glanced inquiringly at Rebecca. "Sure I can't get one for you?"

"I'm holding out for homemade ice cream at the church stand. I heard they have teaberry this year."

"That's for me, then." He wiped his fingers on a napkin. "I don't think the rest of the world has even heard of teaberry ice cream."

Kristie stopped so abruptly that Rebecca almost bumped into her. "Look, Aunt Rebecca." She pointed to the lawn under the maples, where the school boosters had set up games. At the moment a spirited egg-and-spoon race was ending.

"Do you want to be in some of the races?" she asked. "I'll bet they have some just for your age."

Kristie, attacked by shyness, leaned against her, shaking her head.

Brett exchanged a glance with her and then knelt next to the child. "Come on, it'll be fun. I'll hold your candy apple for you."

She looked longingly at the fun, then shook her head again.

"Tell you what. Aunt Rebecca and I will do it first. Then you can give it a try. Okay?"

Kristie's smile appeared. "Okay."

Brett stood, holding out his hand to Rebecca. "Looks like there's a three-legged race starting with our name on it."

It wasn't that she minded joining in the games, especially not if it got Kristie involved. But did it have to be the three-legged race?

Brett bent to tie the strip of cloth around their ankles, binding them so close that it was impossible to keep any distance between them.

"Does it have to be that tight?"

"Unless you want to trip over it, it does." Brett put his arm around her waist. She stiffened, and he raised an eyebrow. "I don't think we can win this if we don't work together."

"Do you always play to win?" She tried, without

success, to still the tingle that danced along her nerve endings everywhere they touched.

His gaze met hers. "Always."

She looked away first. "Maybe we'd better practice."

"Right." Brett hitched his arm more firmly around her. "We have to stay together. Outside step, inside step. Outside, inside."

"Just try it." *And let's get it over with before I start getting used to being so close.*

They'd barely managed to get in a few awkward steps before the starter waved them into position.

Brett's hand tightened at her waist. "This is it. Ready?" He was as eager as if they were launching into the Olympics.

"As ready as I'm going to be," she said, resigned.

The whistle blew, and they started forward.

Outside, inside, outside, inside…she counted the steps as they raced forward, Brett's long strides eating up the ground. He was so intent on the finish line that he almost carried her along.

A rebellious spark ignited. Maybe, for once in his life, it would do Brett good to let someone else win, like the high school kid behind them who was probably trying hard to impress his girlfriend.

It didn't take much, just one mischievous step out of rhythm. Brett stumbled and clutched her for balance. And then they both toppled to the soft grass.

She hadn't anticipated the effect of tumbling to the ground so close to him. His arms went around her protectively, and he twisted so that he hit first. She landed against him, in his arms.

Her breath seemed to stop entirely. For just a moment everything disappeared—the crowds, the music, the laughter. There was nothing on earth but Brett, holding her.

He tightened his grasp. "Rebecca? Are you all right?"

"I will be when you stop squeezing the life out of me." She rolled away from him, tried to get up and was brought back down by the cloth tying their ankles together.

"You can't get away from me no matter how you try." He grinned, reaching down to untie them.

He was right, she thought, trying to get her breathing under control before she had to say anything else. She couldn't get away from him or the way he made her feel, and it didn't matter how many people were around.

Brett balanced the paper bowls of ice cream and worked his way through the crowd to the picnic table under the trees. Rebecca had already settled on a bench next to Kristie. He watched her laugh at something Mitch said, and an uncomfortable jolt of longing swept through him.

How had this happened? When had he started feeling this way about Rebecca? He'd probably been trying to deny it for days, but it wasn't until he'd held her in his arms that he'd actually recognized how desirable she was, and how strongly he was attracted.

This was Rebecca, remember? Little Rebecca. Somehow the reminder didn't do any good. She wasn't "little Rebecca" any longer.

That didn't matter. She was still out of bounds to him. His plans for the future didn't include a serious relationship for a long time. He'd seen too many marriages that didn't survive the pressures of big hospital residencies. That meant he had to get back to thinking of Rebecca as a kid sister, and fast.

He slid a bowl of ice cream in front of her and another in front of Kristie, then found a place on the bench opposite. "I predict a stomachache coming on if she eats all that." He nodded toward Kristie's dish.

"Don't worry, she won't eat much after everything else she's had." Rebecca lifted a spoonful to her lips, then closed her eyes in enjoyment. "Mmm, wonderful."

He took a spoonful of his own, savoring the tart sweetness.

Alex paused, looking at his half-empty bowl. "Do you think we like it so much because it really is that good, or because we only get it once a year?"

Mitch, smiling, threw a balled-up napkin at him. "Quit analyzing, will you? Just enjoy it."

"He can't enjoy it without analyzing it," Brett said. "Never could, never will."

He kept the words light, but he caught the inquiring glance Rebecca threw his way. *Careful.* She already guessed too much about him for comfort.

The conversation bounced around the table, reflecting the easiness of people who knew each other well. He tried to relax and join in, but found he was watching Rebecca, noticing the gentle curve of her cheek, the love in her eyes when she looked at her niece, the way her dimple showed when she laughed. No, it wasn't going to be easy to go back to thinking of Rebecca as a skinny little kid.

Obviously, no one else thought of her that way. The others treated her as a professional, someone worthy of their respect. She was, of course. He'd learned that about her in his time at the clinic. She was good, she was efficient, and most of all she cared. No one came in the clinic door that didn't get one hundred percent from Rebecca.

Kristie pushed her barely touched ice cream away and leaned against her aunt. Her eyelids drooped.

Rebecca put her arm around the child. "What's wrong, sweetie? Are you tired?"

"I can stay up longer." Kristie made a valiant effort to sit up straight. "I'm not tired."

"Maybe you're not, but I am." Brett took a last bite of his ice cream. "And you're my date, so you have to leave when I do."

That made her giggle, erasing the frown from her face. She slid from the bench and took the hand he held out to her.

"Come on, Aunt Rebecca," he said lightly. "Time we called it quits."

"If you want to stay longer..." she began, but he shook his head.

"She's drooping and so am I." He swung Kristie's hand. "We're ready to go."

They said their good-nights and started toward the car. They'd made their way through most of the crowd when a familiar figure stopped in front of them.

"Dr. Elliot." Minna Dawson looked considerably better than she had the last time he'd seen her.

"How are you doing, Mrs. Dawson?" Judging by the way her husband clung to her arm, he must not think she should be wandering around the festival.

"'Bout a hundred times better than I was." She held out her hand. "I've been wanting to stop by and say thank you." A brick-red flush mounted her cheeks. "I wasn't very nice to you, and that's a fact. But seems like you probably saved my life."

He found he was unaccountably touched. "Just doing my job. I'm glad you're better. Did you get started on cardiac rehab?"

She nodded.

"You keep it up, then." Kristie began to drag on his hand, so he picked her up. Her arms looped around his neck. "Have a good time at the festival, but watch what you eat."

"No fear I'll cheat. George won't let me do that." She pressed his hand again. "We'll never forget what you did, Doc. Never."

Rebecca looked at him curiously as they headed on toward the car. "What is it? You look a little stunned. Didn't a patient ever say thank you before?"

He considered the question. "Well, not that many of them. And I certainly never ran into a patient at a social event."

She shrugged. "It happens all the time in a small town. You get used to it."

He wouldn't be around long enough to get used to it. And the thought somehow wasn't pleasant. "She called me 'Doc.'"

"So?" Rebecca lifted an inquiring brow.

He shrugged. "Doc Overton is 'Doc.' I'm just Brett around here."

"Not anymore, you're not." She smiled. "I told you they'd accept you as their doctor."

He thought about that as he drove them home. Bedford Creek accepted him as a doctor, instead of as the class clown he'd once been. It accepted Rebecca, too, as the medical professional she was. Things had changed. Was he the only one who couldn't accept that?

Rebecca had been sure Brett would drop them at the door and be on his way, maybe back to the festival to rejoin his friends. That would certainly be for the best.

But he showed no inclination to do any such thing. Instead he helped tuck Kristie in, then followed Rebecca into the living room and accepted the offer of coffee she felt constrained to make.

She carried the tray in and set it on the coffee table, making up excuses in her mind. It was late; they both had to get up early.

But it wasn't late, and Brett knew perfectly well what time they had to be at the clinic. And he'd settled back on the chintz-covered couch as if he intended to be there for a long time. She sat down at the opposite end and poured the coffee.

"It was good to get together with Mitch and Alex, wasn't it?" She might as well try to find out if her aim for the evening had been successful.

"They're the best." He frowned a little. "I wish…" He stopped.

Something to do with Alex, she was sure. "What is it? I know something's wrong. It's been wrong ever since you saw Alex at the clinic."

She waited for him to tell her it was none of her business, but he just shook his head.

"I talked to Alex about the surgery." His frown deepened, sending harsh vertical lines between his brows. "He's not interested."

"I see." She thought she did see, in a way. "Because of the time he'd have to be away from Bedford Creek, I suppose."

"Why do you say that?" Brett stiffened. "Did he say something to you?"

"No, of course not." She struggled to account for the assumption that had come so easily. "I just thought it might be a problem. He'd have to be away for over a month, probably."

"Isn't that a small price to pay for getting rid of the pain he's having?" Brett demanded.

"I guess it might be to most people. But Alex Caine isn't most people."

"You don't need to tell me that. I'm one of his oldest friends. I know him as well as anyone."

She tried to say what she needed to without hurting him. "Of course you're one of his oldest friends. But you haven't seen him all that much in the last few years."

"I haven't forgotten what he's like, if that's what you're implying."

"He's changed since the accident." She frowned, choosing her words carefully. "Since his wife left. I'm not sure you realize how much."

Brett seemed to bite back his impatience. He probably longed to tell her she didn't know what she was talking about.

"If you know something I don't, I wish you'd tell me. Granted, he took it hard when his wife ran off, but I don't see what that has to do with his recovery from the accident."

"Look, I'm going on my own instincts here, and

maybe I'm wrong." But she didn't think so. "He's carrying a big load of responsibility. He's a single parent, and he's trying hard to be everything to Jason. And he's got the responsibility of the business. Apparently his father left things in a mess when he died shortly after Alex was hurt."

Brett was still frowning, but now it was a thoughtful frown. "He always did take it seriously, owning the business that employs half the town. I can see him deciding to sacrifice his own welfare for everyone else. That's like him." He made a fist. "I want so much to help him."

"Why?" The word was out before she had time to think about it. "I mean, why does it hurt you so much? I know he's your friend, but it seems more than that."

Now he really would tell her to mind her own business. What was she thinking to probe so deeply into his affairs?

Brett leaned forward, hands clenched in front of him. She held her breath, waiting for an explosion, but it didn't come.

"Do you remember anything about the camping-trip accident our senior year?" he asked abruptly. "Or were you too young?"

"Of course I wasn't too young. How do you think I'd forget something the whole town talked about for weeks? You and Mitch and Alex were lucky you weren't killed."

A shiver ran down her spine at the memory. The stories she'd heard had given her nightmare images of the three of them, caught in the abandoned quarry, nearly drowning when the water rose.

"Alex came close." His hands were locked so tight the veins stood out. "If Mitch hadn't pulled him out, he would have died." He looked at her, his eyes very dark. "It was my fault."

"Your fault..." She looked at him blankly. He was serious. "What do you mean, your fault? It was an accident. No one expected the flooding to hit so fast and so hard. That wasn't your fault."

"It was my fault we didn't get back when we were supposed to." He looked past her as if she weren't even there, as if he looked into another time. "I was in charge of the map. I'm the one who lost it. I'm the one who thought it would be great to explore the quarry."

He reeled off his transgressions like an indictment. She didn't know what to say.

Please, Lord, give me the right words. He's really hurting, and I never knew it. I thought I knew him so well, but I didn't know this.

"What do Mitch and Alex think?"

That seemed to break through his abstraction, and he focused on her. "They've never blamed me, if that's what you mean. But I'm still responsible." He shrugged. "For the longest time I couldn't hear the rain without seeing Alex's face when he slipped into the water. If Mitch hadn't grabbed him..."

"Brett." She covered his hand with hers. "You were being a seventeen-year-old kid. You thought you were indestructible. All three of you. But you found out differently. That doesn't make you guilty. It just made you a kid."

"Maybe so. But however you look at it, I owe Alex." He gave her a crooked smile. "I owe the richest man in town, and I thought I'd finally found a way to repay him. But he won't take it."

Her fingers tightened around his. "You have to let him make that decision for himself, Brett. He's the one who knows what's best for him. You wouldn't really want the responsibility of making the decision for him."

For a moment he looked as if he'd argue the point. And then he smiled a genuine smile. "Not even if I think I'm right?"

"Not even if you're the best doctor Bedford Creek has ever produced."

The tension ebbed from his face. "I'm the only doctor Bedford Creek has ever produced, as you well know." He reached out to tug lightly at a strand of her hair. "How did little Rebecca turn out to be so wise?"

He was so close that she could see the fine gold flecks in his eyes, so close she could feel his warm breath on her cheek. All in an instant the air between them had changed, becoming charged with something that made her breath catch.

He seemed to feel it, too. His eyes darkened, and

his hand moved to her cheek. He stroked the line of her jaw, and her skin warmed at his touch. She'd stopped breathing entirely, and surely her heart was too full to beat.

His mouth, sure and warm, found hers. For a fraction of a second she hesitated, held back. Then her arms went around him, drawing him even closer, so close she could feel his heart beat.

Then, abruptly, he pulled away.

She stiffened at the shock on his face.

"I…" He stopped, shook his head. "Good night, Rebecca." He got up and was gone before she could gather her wits to say anything.

She sat for a long time, hand on lips that were still warm from his kiss. Could he have guessed what was in her heart? Was that what had made him long for escape?

She had to hope not. Because she'd fallen in love with Brett Elliot all over again, and sooner or later, she knew he'd leave and break her heart.

Chapter Nine

How much did Brett regret that kiss? That question occupied Rebecca's mind when she arrived at the clinic the next morning. Was *regret* even the right word? Maybe to him it was nothing but a casual kiss between colleagues. Maybe he wouldn't think twice about it.

The trouble was, she really didn't know him any longer. She'd thought she did when he came back, but she'd been wrong. He kept her constantly off balance, far from her usual conviction that she knew exactly where she belonged and what her duty was.

Well, she couldn't sit in the car, staring blankly at nothing. She had to go into the clinic, face him and try to preserve whatever dignity she had left. Because one thing was certain—she didn't want Brett to know what that one kiss had done to her.

She let herself in the back door. The offices slept in early morning silence. Usually she loved this time—loved the chance to get caught up on paperwork, consult with Doc, plan the day's work in peace. Today *peaceful* was the last word to describe her state of mind.

"Rebecca, that you?" Doc poked his head out of his office. "Thought it was. Any coffee?"

She smiled at the familiar greeting. "I'll get it on right away, Doc," she said, as she did every morning. She hesitated, hoping she could sound casual enough. "Brett in yet?"

"Not coming today."

Luckily Doc had disappeared back into his office. His wise old eyes would have seen the surprise she couldn't hide. If Brett wasn't here, where was he? His car had been gone when she left the house this morning. Was this somehow related to what had happened between them the night before?

Nonsense. Brett wouldn't be upset by a little kiss. She started the coffee, then went back to Doc's office. She'd ask, that's all. Surely it was normal for her to want to know why he hadn't come in today.

"Doc? Are you all right?"

He was leaning back in his chair, eyes closed, but he sat up when she said his name. "Fine. Or will be, when I get some coffee."

"You drink too much coffee," she said, as always. "It'll be ready in a minute. Why didn't Brett come in today?"

Doc shrugged. "Just said he had to be out of town for the day. I didn't pry." His tone suggested she shouldn't, either.

So she wouldn't. But that didn't mean she didn't wonder. Brett had left early and apparently expected to be gone the whole day. If it had been an emergency, Doc would have said. So that meant it was something planned, something he had chosen not to mention to her.

The fellowships he'd applied for... The thought gripped her and refused to let go. Her active imagination bolted forward, picturing Brett accepting a fellowship, packing his bags, leaving forever.

It doesn't necessarily mean that. There had to be plenty of other things that would take him out of Bedford Creek for the day. Trouble was, once she started thinking about the fellowship, she couldn't think about anything else.

The day, starting badly, continued to go downhill. The waiting room bubbled with a steady stream of patients. She hadn't realized how much she'd come to depend on Brett until he wasn't there. How had they ever gotten along without him?

Panic gripped her for an instant. How would they get along when he'd gone?

By late afternoon, when Doc had written the wrong prescription for Dean Wagner's insulin and forgotten to suggest an ultrasound for Louise O'Neill, Rebecca felt like a juggler with too many plates in the air. If she hadn't caught Doc's mistakes...

Neither of them was critical, she reminded herself. She had caught them, and no one else needed to know. But she drove home determined to wait on Brett's front porch as long as necessary, until he came back and she could demand to know what he was doing.

As it turned out, no such measure was necessary. When she pulled into the driveway under a canopy of red maples, Brett was just pulling into his drive on the other side of the hedge. They got out of their cars simultaneously.

Without stopping to think about it, Rebecca pushed through the gap in the hedge she'd been using since she was old enough to walk.

"Rebecca. Hi."

Brett looked... She wasn't sure how to describe his expression. Pleased about something, maybe that was it.

She thought of the fellowship, and panic gripped her again. He wouldn't look that happy unless they'd offered it to him.

"Where have you been?" Fear made her abrupt.

He raised his eyebrows at her tone. "No polite greeting? No asking how my day went?"

"I know how your day went. You look like the cat that swallowed the canary. Where were you?"

Brett pulled a briefcase from the back seat and

slammed the door. He nodded toward the house. "Come on in, and I'll tell you."

Being alone with Brett was probably the last thing she ought to do. But it was the only way she'd find out the truth. She followed him into the house.

Brett led the way to the living room. He put his briefcase on the cherry coffee table and opened it, taking out a sheaf of papers clipped together. "Take a look at this." He shoved them into her hands.

"What is it?"

He threw himself into the armchair across from her, loosening his tie. "I don't know how people manage to wear these things all day. Felt like I was choking." He nodded toward the papers in her hand. "Go on, read through that. I want your opinion."

If he wanted her opinion on a fellowship offer, he wouldn't like what he got. She sank down on the couch and started to read. After a moment she looked at Brett.

"This is a physical-therapy plan."

He nodded. "For Alex." He seemed to register her surprise. "Why? What did you think it was?"

"Nothing. It doesn't matter," she said quickly. She shuffled through the papers. "This is very comprehensive. Where did you get it?"

"Philadelphia." He leaned back, yawning. "A buddy of mine from med school runs an orthopedic clinic that's got a state-of-the-art therapy program.

I took him Alex's records and asked him to design a treatment plan. What do you think?''

She took her time, leafing through the papers, checking out the detailed charts. Finally she looked up again.

"I think it looks excellent. Unfortunately, I also think you won't get Alex to go to Philadelphia for treatment."

He gestured impatiently. "I don't intend to. That's the whole point. He won't take the time a decent therapy program would require, so I'm going to bring the program to him."

"Bring it to him," she echoed. She had to admit, he had a point. She'd tried without success to get Alex to attend sessions even twice weekly at the regional hospital. He'd gone once or twice, then dropped it, saying he couldn't afford the time to drive forty miles each way.

"That's right." Brett's eyes danced with contagious enthusiasm. "Believe me, I'm going to make it impossible for him to say no."

"But how? If he won't go to a clinic—" She gestured with the papers. "Bedford Creek doesn't even have a health club. No one in town has this kind of equipment."

"Leave it to me. I've got a plan that can't fail." He raised an eyebrow. "You in to help?"

He obviously wanted to keep his scheme a secret. "Yes, of course I'll help." She stood, holding the papers out to him. "I'll make a couple of copies of that at the office tomorrow, if you want, so I can study it more closely.''

He got up, looking at her with a quizzical expression as he took the papers. "You seem to be in a hurry."

She took a step toward the door. "I have things to do."

And staying here, thinking about how devastating Brett looked when he was excited about something, was definitely not a good idea. He apparently intended to ignore what had happened between them the night before, so she would, too.

He closed the gap between them. "You seem a little stiff. You're not mad at me for taking the day off, are you? It was for a good cause."

"No, of course not." If only he wouldn't stand so close to her, she'd find it easier to keep her tone light and unflustered.

"Then it has to be last night. Am I in the doghouse for stealing a kiss from an old friend?"

The light words cut her to the heart. That's all she was to Brett. All she'd ever be. *An old friend.*

Her only choice was to play along and pretend it meant as little to her as it obviously did to him. The trouble was, she wasn't sure she could succeed—not with his intent gaze fixed on her face.

"When did anyone ever manage to keep you in the doghouse?" She managed a smile. "You always charmed your way out." She spun, holding on to the smile with an effort. "I really have to go. I'll see you tomorrow."

"I'm telling you, Mitch, it's never going to fit." Brett looked from the beat-up chest to the attic stairway late the following afternoon. "We'll break our necks trying to get it up those narrow steps."

"Wimp," Mitch teased, grinning. "Come on, let's see what you're made of. I promised Anne I'd have that room cleaned out and ready for Emilie, and that's what I'm going to do."

"If it kills me," Brett grumbled, but he hefted one end of the chest. "Okay, let's give it a try."

At least moving furniture was a change from his current worry. No, make that plural—worries. Rebecca and Doc.

The chest made it halfway through the narrow doorway, then stuck. He looked at Mitch over its top. "I told you so."

"Put your back into it," Mitch advised. He gave a shove, and the chest popped through, nearly flattening Brett in the process.

He rubbed his shoulder. "If you disable me, what's Bedford Creek going to do for medical care?"

"Same as it always has," Mitch said. They hoisted the chest the rest of the way to the dusty attic. "Depend on Doc."

"How long do you think that can last?" It was on the tip of his tongue to mention the hospital's proposal to Mitch, but he bit it back. He shouldn't talk to anyone else about it until he'd talked to Doc.

Mitch shoved the chest against a wall, wiped his forehead and looked at Brett, eyes narrowing. "Why? What's wrong?"

Rebecca was the one he should talk to about this particular problem, but talking to Rebecca had become difficult. They'd worked together with patients and on the therapy plan for Alex, but she'd been consistently evasive, slipping away every time there was a chance they might be alone.

He had to talk to someone, and he could trust Mitch's discretion. "I'm worried about Doc."

Mitch leaned against the chest, looking ready to stay there all day, if necessary. "What's wrong with Doc, other than being overworked?"

"I'm not sure." He frowned. "Maybe it's nothing. People do make mistakes. Even doctors."

"No, really?" Mitch mimicked astonishment. "I thought you guys took lessons from Superman."

Brett punched his arm, as he'd have done back in high school. It was like hitting a brick wall.

"Guess that's how I think about Doc. That he shouldn't make mistakes."

Mitch sobered. "And he has?"

"Nothing big. Nothing either Rebecca or I didn't catch." He wondered how many other errors Rebecca had caught and corrected without saying anything. "I just…it worries me," he admitted.

"You're sure they were errors? I mean, not just something you might have done differently?"

"No." He thought of the blank look on Doc's face when he'd mentioned Mrs. Clancy's blood pressure. "These were mistakes a raw intern wouldn't make."

Mitch didn't respond for a minute, his face impassive. Brett knew that guarded look. It meant Mitch was struggling with something unpalatable.

"You think it's just that he's worn out?" he said finally. "Or you think it's something more serious?"

A fly buzzed lazily in a patch of sunlight from the attic window, and Brett took out his frustration by swatting at it. "Wish I knew. I've been trying to get Doc to let me do a thorough physical exam, but he always has an excuse."

"What does Rebecca say?"

The other part of his problem loomed. "I haven't talked to Rebecca about it."

Mitch looked astonished. "Why not? If anyone knows what's going on with Doc, it's Rebecca."

"Rebecca and I haven't been doing a lot of talking lately." *Not since I kissed her.* No, he couldn't say that to Mitch. Back when they were in high school, maybe—but not now.

"Why not?" Mitch's eyes narrowed. "You haven't hurt her feelings, have you? Treated her like she's still a little kid?"

That was the least of his problems. "Not at all.

It's just that Rebecca thinks it's my duty to stay, so she suspects everything I say about Doc. You know Rebecca—she's a great one for doing your duty.''

"Nothing wrong with that.'' Mitch, with his background in the military, set a high value on duty, Brett knew.

Brett lifted an eyebrow. "Does that mean you think I should stay, too?''

"I think it's between you and Doc,'' Mitch said firmly. "And nobody else's business.''

Except God's. He suspected that was what Mitch was thinking, but wouldn't say. Mitch didn't believe in preaching to his friends, but the way he lived his life made his own beliefs clear.

Mitch clapped him on the shoulder. "Come on, let's get back to work. If you take my advice, you'll talk to Rebecca about it.'' He nodded toward the stairwell. "You'll have a chance soon. That's her with Anne now.''

"I've got the border, but we need a pail of water.'' Rebecca looked back at Anne, who carried brushes and a plastic drop cloth.

"I'll get it.'' Anne dropped her load in the second-floor hall of Mitch's house. She glanced over Rebecca's shoulder. "Or better yet, Brett can get it.''

"Brett.'' She swung around, nearly losing the rolls of wallpaper border she carried. Brett and Mitch had evidently just come through the attic door. Brett had a smudge of dust on his cheek, and she resisted the urge to wipe it away. "I didn't expect to see you here."

And didn't want to. She'd spent the last couple of days avoiding him, at least as much as it was possible to in a small office. Now here he was, and she'd committed herself to working on the baby's room with Anne.

"Just helping Mitch move some things."

He seemed ill at ease, which surprised her. Cool, confident Brett was never ill at ease.

"We'd better get it finished," Mitch pointed out. "The women want to work in there."

Anne smiled up at him. "We wouldn't object to some help."

Yes, we would, Rebecca thought, but there was no use saying it. Mitch would be delighted to help Anne do absolutely anything, and neither Brett nor she could back out gracefully now. It looked as if they were destined to spend the next several hours together.

Brett waved toward the door. "After you."

She tried to imagine a clear glass wall between herself and Brett—a nice barrier to let her stay detached. It didn't work. Even her imagination wasn't good enough to achieve that.

She dropped the rolls of border on a stack of newspaper and glanced around the small room. "This is going to be perfect for Emilie." She knelt on the padded window seat, looking out at the apple tree in the backyard. "What did you use it for, Mitch?"

"Officially, a guest room." Mitch picked up a box and shoved it into Brett's arms. "Actually, it turned into a catch-all. But don't worry. Brett and I will have the rest of this out of the way in no time."

"No time, he says." Brett staggered toward the door. "I'll just run right up the attic steps with this thing. What do you have in here, rocks?"

Mitch grinned. "And after we get this cleared, we'll bring up the baby's furniture from the garage." He hoisted another box and followed the sound of Brett's groan.

Anne's deep blue eyes clouded with worry. "I told Mitch I thought we should use movers instead of imposing on his friends."

"Don't be silly. Brett wants to help. Besides, it will do him good to do some manual labor for once."

"A little hard on him, aren't you?" Anne looked at her questioningly. "Or is that a smoke screen for what you really feel?"

Rebecca felt her cheeks warm, and she bent to pick up the tape measure. "I don't know what you mean. Are you thinking of new curtains in here?"

The conversation returned to decorating, and she tried not to think about how she must be giving her feelings away. Even Anne, who'd known her for months instead of years, could tell. She had to get a grip, or Brett might start suspecting something.

At least Mitch's and Anne's presence would preclude any private conversations with Brett. She could handle this. They were a work party, not a double date.

And she did handle it, keeping the conversation light and general while they put up the fanciful animal border. Everything went fine, right up until the moment when both Anne and Mitch vanished downstairs on separate errands, leaving her alone with Brett.

She concentrated on the last bit of border, smoothing out an invisible wrinkle from a smiling bunny. She felt, rather than saw, Brett's approach.

"Looks nice." He stopped inches from her step stool. "I didn't know you were a paper-hanger, too. Is there anything you can't do?"

"Plenty." She hopped down from the stool, putting a few additional inches between herself and Brett. "Too many to list. Maybe I'd better see if Anne needs any help."

Brett stood between her and the door. "Just a second. I want to talk to you."

"Can it wait? I want—"

"No, it can't wait." He frowned. "I've been trying to have a serious conversation with you, but you always manage to slip away."

That was true enough, but she hadn't known he noticed. Tension shivered along her nerves. If Brett wanted a serious conversation, it couldn't be about anything good. Had his fellowship come through? Or was it something more personal?

"I'm here now." She crossed her arms protectively. "What is it?"

His frown deepened. "What's wrong with Doc?"

The attack came out of the blue, and she wasn't prepared for it. "What do you mean?"

"Don't pretend you don't know what I'm talking about." He transferred the frown to her. "You know as well as I do that something's wrong with him."

"I don't..." She let the words die. Denying it wouldn't help. "All right, he forgets things now and then. He's working too hard."

"How long have you been covering up his mistakes?"

So Brett had noticed. "That's why I'm there, to pick up on those little things."

"Not so little, Rebecca." His tone was somber. "The things I've noticed weren't minor, by any means. And I'm wondering how many other things I *didn't* see." He leaned closer to her, face intent. "Come on, level with me."

She was caught again, between what she wanted to do and her promise to Doc. She took a deep breath. She'd have to trust Brett with some of the truth and hope he used it wisely.

"It's been about a year." She turned away, staring out the window so she wouldn't have to look at Brett. "I've noticed him failing for about the last year."

"A year?" he echoed. "And you haven't done anything about it?"

She was too upset to be angry at his tone. "At first it really was forgetting just little things. But it's gotten worse lately." Her throat tightened. "I don't know what to do."

She felt his hands on her shoulders, warm and strong.

"Well, the first thing you have to do is not try to carry everything yourself. It's not just your problem, you know."

"In a way, it is. There's no other medical professional I can turn to. I thought, when you came back..." She stopped, unable to go on.

"You thought I'd take over." His hands dropped from her shoulders. "I've already told you that's not going to happen. But that doesn't mean I don't care about Doc. Has he seen another doctor?"

She managed a smile. "You know the answer to that one. Of course not, no matter what I say. I even made an appointment for him, but he cancelled it."

"Stubborn old coot." Affection filled the words, so that she couldn't take offense. "What do you think is wrong? You must have an opinion."

This was where it got difficult. She could only hope he'd understand. "All I know is what I've observed, because he hasn't let me run any tests."

She turned so that she could see his face. "And Doc made me promise not to discuss his health with anyone. Including you."

"Are you saying you won't tell me what you've seen?" He sounded as if he doubted her sanity.

"Brett, please understand. I promised Doc. How can I break my word?"

His eyes flashed. "That's plain stupid. How am I going to help him if you won't tell me what's wrong?"

"You've seen the same things I have." Her anger sparked in return.

"I haven't been here as long as you have, Rebecca. I don't like working in the dark."

"Then why don't you insist on giving him a physical?"

"I'll do that, but it would help to know what you think." He glared at her, baffled and angry.

It *was* stupid, that was all she could think, echoing Brett's word. Stupid that the two of them, who loved Doc, were incapable of helping him.

Her anger ebbed, replaced by worry. She reached toward him tentatively, willing him to understand. "Think about it, Brett. You know if he'd made you promise, you'd feel the same way."

"That's different." His response was quick.

"Why? Because you're the doctor?"

His face was tight, holding his anger against her. For a long moment, he didn't say anything, and then he shook his head.

"All right. I guess I can understand why you don't want to betray his confidence. I'll try and get him to let me do a thorough work-up. But if he won't..."

He paused, and her heart seemed to stop.

"If he won't, I'll have no choice but to talk to the clinic board. I don't want to, but I will."

Chapter Ten

Was there anything else she could have said to Brett? Rebecca still worried about it the following morning as she puttered around the house doing her usual Saturday morning chores. They both wanted what was best for Doc, didn't they?

Unfortunately, they probably wouldn't ever agree on what that was. If Brett pushed Doc too hard about a checkup; if Doc got his back up and wouldn't let Brett examine him; if Brett made good on his threat to go to the clinic board...

Her thoughts went round and round. What could she do? There had to be a way to resolve this that wouldn't hurt Doc.

Maybe if she talked to him seriously, told him how worried Brett was, how worried they both were—maybe then he'd see that he couldn't just keep stonewalling everyone about the state of his health.

She paused, arms full of a load of laundry. Doc usually went to the office on Saturday morning, even though he didn't see patients then, to catch up on paperwork. This might be the perfect opportunity to talk with him in an unhurried way before Brett tackled him about a checkup. It could be her only chance to smooth the way, so she'd better take it.

Half an hour later she'd changed clothes and started for the clinic. But she'd forgotten, in her worry, that the festival was still going on. The streets were crowded with people determined to enjoy themselves.

It took her extra time to get to the clinic, but when she arrived, Doc's battered station wagon was the only vehicle in the parking lot. She unlocked the back door and went quietly in.

Doc sat at his desk, a file open in front of him, but he didn't seem to be reading it. He leaned back, eyes closed, and tears slipped down his cheeks.

She felt a stab of pain in her heart. "Doc, what is it?" She hurried to his side. "Are you all right?"

He jerked upright, startled, and then wiped at the tears with the back of his hand. He fumbled for the glasses he'd pushed to the top of his head, sliding them into place like a barricade.

"All right? Why wouldn't I be all right? What are you doing here?"

Her heart started beating again when she heard his usual testy tone. "I came in to see you." She took his hand, conscious of the fragility of the hands that had once been so strong. "What is it, Doc? Please tell me what's wrong. You were crying."

He shook his head irritably, then snatched up a tissue and mopped his face. "Allergies, that's all."

"You've never had an allergic reaction in your life."

Somehow she had to make him level with her. They just couldn't go on this way. She leaned across to look at the file, realizing with a sense of shock that it was her father's.

He must have seen the expression in her eyes. He fumbled with the folder, sliding it into the desk drawer.

"Why did you have that out, Doc?" She tried to keep emotion from her voice. "That's been over with a long time."

For a moment she thought he'd try to dismiss it.

Then he shook his head. "Just thinking. Wondering."

"Wondering what?"

He fidgeted with the drawer pull. "If I'd missed something. If I should have caught it sooner. Maybe…"

Panic clutched her. That was what she'd been feeling for two years, but she'd never realized Doc was going through the same thing. Brett's words came back to her. Every medical professional does that—blame himself.

"Oh, Doc." Her voice was thick. "You know everyone thinks that when they've lost someone they love. Especially medical personnel. We think we should have been able to save them." She put her arms around him, resting her cheek against his head. "But we can't save everyone. We're not God."

I'm sorry, Daddy. I'm sorry. The pain she hadn't realized was still hiding in her own heart flared for an instant, then seemed to ease.

For a long moment Doc held her as if she were his lifeline. Then he pulled back, clearing his throat, probably embarrassed by the unusual show of emotion.

Unusual. The word reverberated in her mind. It was unusual, yet another piece of the puzzle she and Brett had to unravel somehow.

"I need to get back to work," Doc said gruffly. "And you've got better things to do with your Saturday than hang around here."

She leaned against the desk. "I'm not leaving until I have your promise. Doc, you've got to let Brett give you a thorough going over. You've got to. And you might as well give in, because I won't."

"That's good advice, Doc."

She spun to find Brett standing in the doorway. He came toward them, face determined.

How long had he been standing there? Had he heard her repeating his own words?

Doc looked from Brett to her. "You two ganging up on me?"

"We didn't plan to," Brett said. "But we're both worried about you, Doc, so you might as well make up your mind to go along with us."

She touched Doc's shoulder. "We love you, you know. It's not right to shut us out like this. Give us a chance to help you."

Doc's eyes closed, as if he had to withdraw from the two of them a bit. Was he remembering his grief over not healing her father? Did he realize how much they needed the chance to help him?

Please, Lord. Please.

She glanced at Brett, willing him to give Doc the time to decide, and had the quick impression he was praying, too.

Doc looked up at them finally, weary but somehow resigned. "I guess if I've got to trust my health to someone, it might as well be the two of you." He stood, shrugging off his jacket. "Let's get on with it."

Brett was as coolly professional as if Doc were a patient he'd just met for the first time. She stayed in the background, helping as unobtrusively as possible, but she couldn't stop her busy mind.

What was Brett thinking? Of the same possibilities that had haunted her in recent weeks—Parkinson's, impending stroke? Or something she hadn't even thought of?

When he'd finished, Brett stood looking down at the chart, frowning. He transferred the frown to Doc. "You know what I'm going to say is the next step. It's the same thing you'd say to a patient with your symptoms."

Doc's face tightened. "You want me to see a neurologist for a complete work-up. But I don't—"

"That's what you'd recommend, isn't it?" Brett interrupted firmly.

Stubborn silence ensued. Finally Doc nodded.

Rebecca discovered she could breathe again. "I'll call and make the appointment."

"Maybe next month, when we're not so busy," Doc began.

"As soon as I can get you in," she said. "And you're going, if we have to tie you down and take you there."

Doc divided a glare between the two of them, but it lacked his usual fierceness. "Guess you two think you're pretty smart, don't you?"

Brett put his arm across Doc's shoulder. "If we are, we both know who to blame it on." He glanced at Rebecca, as if reminding her they were in this together. "We went into medicine because of you, both of us."

"Now, you just keep turning that," Pastor Richie said, his blue eyes twinkling, "and we'll have the best batch of homemade ice cream at the festival.''

Brett couldn't help but smile back at the man who'd been his pastor since he was a kid. Cranking ice cream wasn't how he'd planned to spend the last night of the festival, but it was tough to say no to Pastor Richie. At least he didn't have to serve the dishes and cones. Rebecca had been drafted to do that.

He glanced at her as she handed a top-heavy cone to a small boy. So far he'd managed to evade her questions about Doc, but that couldn't last forever. Now that the whole thing was in the open, sooner or later they'd have to discuss the possibilities. But he had a respite as long as the steady stream of customers kept her busy.

Unfortunately, turning a crank on the ice-cream maker left his mind free to worry about Doc. He frowned. Had he done all the right things?

He had, of course he had. But he was discovering it wasn't so easy to be satisfied with your actions when the patient was someone you cared about.

He pictured Doc the way he'd seen him at the office, agonizing about the care he'd given Rebecca's father. Two years later, and still he worried over whether he'd done the right thing. Would that be him, two years from now, berating himself because he imagined he'd missed something with Doc?

The ice cream must be stiffening, because the

handle grew suddenly harder to turn. He put his muscles into it, expending the energy he didn't want to spend worrying.

This was what it was like, being a general practitioner in your own hometown. Knowing people too well, worrying about them, fearing that maybe you hadn't done your best. It added an emotional layer to medicine that he didn't like. Far better to be detached, able to turn off the thoughts when the shift was over.

"Brett's doing a batch of chocolate now," he heard Rebecca tell someone.

She glanced toward him. "Is that almost done? I'm getting requests from the chocoholics."

"Getting there." He shoved the handle, muscles straining. "How do you tell when it's ready?"

"By the feel of it." Rebecca knelt beside him, putting her hands next to his on the crank and giving it an experimental turn. "I'd say another minute or two will do."

Easy for her to say. She wasn't the one who had to finish it.

He let his gaze rest on Rebecca as she returned to the counter to try and convince three teenage girls they really wanted peach. He could sense the mixture of relief and worry she tried to hide. Relief that they were finally getting help for Doc; worry at what that help would entail.

At least there was a well-known neurologist at the regional hospital. He'd rather have taken Doc to Philadelphia, but Doc had vetoed that suggestion out of hand.

Well, maybe it was for the best. Maybe being at Lincoln Medical Center as a patient would alleviate some of the antagonism Doc had toward the hospital and the clinics it ran. He'd assumed Doc wouldn't want to go there, wouldn't want the medical center having any additional ammunition for use in taking over the clinic. But Doc seemed resigned to it.

He glanced toward Rebecca again. He should take the opportunity to sound her out about those clinics. She undoubtedly had an opinion very similar to Doc's. And he could hardly badger Doc about it while he was waiting out his appointment with the specialist.

"Okay, Rebecca, I think this is ready." He hefted the ice-cream maker to the table. "I'm making no guarantees, though."

She lifted the lid.

"Maybe we'd better make you taste it first, just to be sure it's safe." She scooped up a plastic spoonful and held it to his lips. "What do you think?"

He held it on his tongue for a moment, savoring the sweet coldness. "Best ice cream I ever tasted."

She lifted an eyebrow. "You might be prejudiced."

"Try it yourself." He dipped a spoon in and held it out to her.

Smiling, she took the spoonful. He managed to get a dab of it on her chin, and wiped it off with his finger. Her skin was warm and smooth, and he suddenly realized how close they stood in the small booth.

Apparently she did, too, because she backed up, bumping against the counter. "That's...that's very good." She turned away. "Let's get the chocolate lovers served."

But the chocolate lovers seemed to have vanished.

Pastor Richie popped back into the booth. "Everyone's finding a spot to watch the fireworks." He picked up the container of chocolate, sliding it into the freezer. "We won't have any customers until the show is over, so you two might as well go watch."

"I don't need—" Rebecca began, but the pastor made shooing motions with his hands.

"Go, go on now, both of you." He shepherded them out of the booth. "Take her on the bridge, Brett. You'll get the best view from there."

Brett smiled at Rebecca's expression. "You might as well give up and watch the fireworks. You know what he's like once he gets an idea. We'll never hear the end of it if we don't go out on the bridge."

Rebecca nodded, falling into step with him.

Plenty of other people had the same idea, but the bridge across the river was long enough for them to spread out. He found a spot about halfway down and leaned his elbows on the rail. In the distance, the high school band tuned up.

Rebecca hesitated a moment, then leaned against the rail next to him. "It's beautiful, isn't it?" She lifted her face to the breeze that swept along the river, letting it ruffle the bronze curls around her face.

"Beautiful," he agreed. Then he turned to look at the view. Well, it was beautiful, too.

The river stretched like a sheet of pewter, glistening in the dusk. Along its edges, the shadows of the trees made a black border that rustled and moved, wavering on the surface of the water.

"First star," Rebecca said softly.

He glanced up. One pale star flickered in a gray-blue sky. The western ridge was purple, the more distant mountains shading away until he wasn't sure whether he could see them or not.

His throat went tight. Rebecca was right. It was beautiful. He'd just been too preoccupied most of the time to notice.

"They're going to play 'Yankee Doodle' first," she predicted, nodding toward the band that was arranging itself on a makeshift stage by the riverbank.

"How do you know?" He leaned a little closer, his elbow brushing hers.

She smiled. "Because they always do. If there's one thing you can be sure of, it's that the band will start with 'Yankee Doodle' and end with the '1812 Overture.'"

The strains of 'Yankee Doodle' floated across the water. "You win," he said, clasping her hand.

She didn't pull away. Somehow the events of the morning had made them…friends? Colleagues? Allies? He wasn't sure what, but he knew they were closer now than they'd ever been.

She glanced up at him. "Thinking about Doc?"

"In a way, I guess." He stared out at the water, watching a bat swoop low over the shining surface. "It's hard not to."

Her hand tensed under his. "I know you don't want to guess. But what do you think they're going to find?"

She was right. He didn't want to guess. "If I knew that, I wouldn't have to send him to a neurologist."

"You must have an idea."

"You can fill in the blanks as well as I can, Rebecca." His fingers tightened on hers. "Now that it's out in the open, you can level with me. Is there anything you've noticed that Doc didn't tell me?"

She shook her head, giving a little sigh. "Nothing. Brett, you don't know how relieved I am. I wanted all along to talk to you about it, but how could I? I'd promised."

Stubborn, responsible Rebecca, with her loving heart and her strict sense of honor. He wouldn't want her to be any different.

"I know," he said. "It's okay. Now…" He tried to find something reassuring to say. "We just have to hope for the best. I've heard good things about this Dr. Morrisey he's seeing."

"I have, too." She frowned. "I know you wanted him to go to Philadelphia, but Morrisey has an excellent reputation."

This might be his chance to sound her out about the medical center. "We're lucky there's a tertiary care hospital only forty miles away. Plenty of people have to go farther than that."

"I guess so." She stared out at the water, her voice noncommittal.

"I heard the hospital took over a practice in Henderson and set up a clinic there." *Maybe they'll do that here.* No, he wasn't ready to say that yet. Not until he'd talked to Doc about it.

She swung to face him. "You know what they did there?" she demanded, her tone already telling him she hadn't approved, whatever it was.

"Something you didn't like, obviously."

She ignored that. "They retired the two doctors who were in practice there originally. Then they staffed the clinic with residents, who rotated in and out every few months. Imagine! Every time you go in, you have a different doctor."

It didn't seem strange to him, but Rebecca was used to care from the doctor who'd delivered her. "That's not really so unusual," he ventured.

"It is around here." She frowned at him. "I suppose that's an example of big-city medicine."

"Family-medicine residents have to gain experience somewhere." He didn't think she'd be convinced.

"Well, not here," she said tartly. "I'm glad Bedford Creek is too small to interest the medical center. They've been buying up practices all over the area, but they wouldn't want to set up in a town this size. I suppose it wouldn't pay."

Not unless the Bedford Creek clinic were folded into a larger one. Then it would pay very well. He considered telling her about the hospital's plan... considered it and rejected it.

He had to talk to Doc first, that was clear. And since Doc apparently hadn't confided in Rebecca about the offers he'd already turned down, the situation was doubly difficult.

A preliminary *crack* sounded from the fireworks staging area. "They're starting." Rebecca swung back toward the view, her voice as eager as a child's.

A rocket whooshed into the night sky, sending out a shower of red and blue flares. Rebecca grasped his hand, and he heard her gasp.

"Oh, how beautiful." She looked up at him, eyes shining. "I just love fireworks, don't you?"

Actually, he'd never thought all that much about fireworks. But anything that could wipe the worry from Rebecca's eyes had his vote.

"Love them," he said firmly.

Another one shot across the darkening sky, this time arcing so low that the sparks actually fell into the water.

"Now you see why they do it over the river," Rebecca said. She leaned closer to him, shivering a little as the breeze freshened.

He put his arm around her, feeling the gentle curve of her shoulders. She leaned against him, relaxed and trusting for perhaps the first time since he'd come back.

Trusting. The word echoed in his thoughts. He might as well enjoy this moment, because it wouldn't last long. Sooner or later they'd clash again, about Doc, about the clinic, about what the future was meant to be. And when they did, the fireworks weren't going to be nearly as pretty as these.

Chapter Eleven

Too many things had been conspiring to keep him focused on Bedford Creek. Brett picked up the telephone on Monday morning with a fresh sense of purpose. He hadn't followed through with a phone call about the Chicago fellowship because he'd been so preoccupied with Doc, the clinic, his patients, and everything else that was going on.

With Rebecca, a little voice whispered in his mind. *You've been thinking about Rebecca.*

It was time he stopped that particular useless line of thought. He and Rebecca weren't destined to be anything other than friends. In fact, when he left Bedford Creek she'd probably no longer consider him even a friend.

There was definitely no future in thinking about how her incredible amber eyes mirrored her every thought—sparkling when she laughed, flashing when she was angry with him, warm with concern when she looked at patients, filled with love at the sight of Kristie. He didn't think he'd ever known a woman who could say so much with a single look, and the funny thing was that she didn't even realize it.

When she'd leaned against his shoulder while they watched the fireworks from the bridge, he'd experienced a mix of emotions that alarmed him. He didn't think he'd ever felt quite that way before—a jumble of protectiveness, tenderness, desire, longing...

Enough. He was shaken all over again just remembering it. A good antidote to his pointless feelings for Rebecca was to call the Chicago program and find out the status of his fellowship. That would remind him of where his priorities ought to be. He couldn't achieve the future he dreamed of without intense, single-minded focus on his objectives. And that meant no wandering off to remember how soft Rebecca's lips had been against his.

Fifteen minutes later he hung up the phone, somewhat startled at how quickly his mission had been accomplished. Not only was his application still in the running, but they wanted him for an interview, as soon as possible. He'd had trouble putting them off until the following week.

Predictable, he thought, unable to suppress a grin. They hadn't bothered to call him, but they wanted him to drop everything and rush to Chicago at a moment's notice.

But he couldn't. All those responsibilities he'd been thinking about interfered. Doc's tests were this week, and he wouldn't leave without knowing the results. And Mitch's wedding was coming up on Saturday. The earliest he could possibly be there was Monday, so that would have to do.

He'd sensed the promise in the voice of the program head. If the interview went well, there was every chance the fellowship would be his.

He should be happy. He was happy. But still… He frowned out the front window at his mother's flower bed. He'd changed since he'd returned to Bedford Creek. Maybe the change had started earlier, back in Philadelphia, the moment he faced the decision to treat that homeless patient. He'd suddenly felt a need to make a decision because it was God's plan, not just because it was best for him.

So was this fellowship God's plan for him? It was a difficult question to ask, because he had to take the answer seriously.

Most of his colleagues back in Philly wouldn't even consider the question. They'd make a decision based on career advantage, and that was it. Rebecca, of course, probably asked that question first. Just thinking about her made him think about how seldom he'd consciously taken God's will into account.

How did anyone know what God's will was in a

particular situation? Too bad Pastor Richie hadn't covered the topic in Sunday's sermon.

His medical talent was a gift from God—that he was sure of. That was one belief that had been bedrock all his life. He'd known instinctively that whatever gifts he had, God was the source. Wouldn't God expect him to use those gifts to the fullest?

The fellowship in Chicago would certainly do that. He'd be working with some of the best surgeons in the country. His excitement grew at the thought. He might actually be the one chosen. Surely that meant it was the path he should follow.

Rebecca wouldn't agree. The thought slipped into his mind, and he had to make a conscious effort to eject it.

It didn't matter what Rebecca thought. She wasn't a determining factor in his future.

Rebecca looked doubtfully at the load of equipment Brett proposed unloading at the Caine mansion. It had taken a rented van to get it all here. Now she, Brett and Mitch were going to set up Alex's very own treatment facility.

"Does Alex know all this is coming?" She stepped back out of the way as Mitch opened the van door.

Brett grinned, taking one end of the heavy carton Mitch was pulling out. "He hasn't a clue," he said.

"I didn't know what he'd say if I told him, so I didn't tell him."

She stared at him, not knowing whether to laugh or not. "What if he tells us to turn right around and take it away again?"

"He won't do that." He nodded toward a smaller box. "You bring that one."

She picked it up with an effort. It was heavier than it looked. "How do you know he won't kick us out?"

"Because he's not here." He flashed her that self-confident grin. "I talked Maida Hansen into co-operating with us. She'll let us in, and she cleared out a room for us to use."

Everyone knew that Maida, the Caine family's longtime housekeeper, was devoted to Alex. If Maida thought standing on her head would help Alex get better, that's what she'd do. She probably hadn't even questioned Brett.

Well, it wasn't Rebecca's job to question, either. She followed the two men up the three steps to the portico that swept around the mansion. Surely, in a house this size, it hadn't been a problem to find an empty room to put the equipment. Whether Alex would agree to the program was another question.

Maida held open the double doors whose frosted glass panels bore an etched *C*. Old Mr. Caine had been proud of his name, so people said.

"This way." Maida ushered them in and glanced back down the sweep of the circular drive, her angular face lined with worry. "Mr. Alex shouldn't be back for an hour, but I don't know."

"Now, Maida." Brett let Mitch support the weight of the box while he patted Maida's shoulder. "You know we're doing the right thing. Even if Alex complains, this is for his own good."

Her mouth set in firm lines. "It's high time he did something for his own good, that's for sure. You just tell me what to do to make him better. I'll do it."

"That's the spirit." Brett took the end of the carton again. "Okay, let's get rolling. We're going to have a fitness center set up for Alex by the time he walks through the door."

"I'm going to need a massage by then," Mitch said. "Can I put this down yet?"

"In here." Maida hurried to push open another door. "Will this room be all right?"

"Perfect," Brett said.

Rebecca nodded, glancing around. Maida had picked the old conservatory, empty of plants now that there was apparently no one with the time or interest to look after them. Even empty, the room was charming, with its bank of windows and French doors opening onto the patio at the rear of the house. Given the size of the Caine estate, Alex would have perfect privacy for his workouts, in spite of all the windows.

Mitch ripped open the first carton. "You want to set this up before we bring in the next?"

Brett nodded. "At least that way we'll have something to show Alex, in case he comes back before we're done."

She looked at him sharply. Maybe Mitch didn't hear it, but she did. There was an undertone of tension in Brett's voice that told her clearly what he was thinking and feeling.

This was his way of paying Alex back. In some obscure, masculine way of keeping accounts, he felt he'd been left owing Alex a debt for his part, however innocent, in the camping accident. He wouldn't be happy until he'd figured out a way to repay that debt.

Men, she decided as she opened the box she'd brought in, were strange creatures. She glanced again at the two of them, engrossed in putting together the fitness machine.

They both wore jeans and T-shirts, but it wouldn't matter what Mitch wore. He always looked like a cop. She'd never figured out exactly what it was that conveyed that, but she knew it was true. As for Brett...

Her heart gave its usual *thump* when she looked at him. The man was dangerous to her self-control, unfortunately. Jeans and a white T-shirt emblazoned with a Run for Your Heart logo didn't do a thing to detract from his appeal. His skin glowed with good health, and the muscles that rippled as he wrestled the machine into place declared that he took fitness seriously.

He glanced across at her. His gaze held hers for a long moment, during which her heart forgot to beat. Then he smiled, slowly. Devastatingly. She forced herself to frown intently down at the contents of her box, as if engrossed in putting whatever it was together. In fact, she hadn't a clue what it was—and if Brett didn't stop looking at her she felt as if she'd self-destruct.

"What do you think, Rebecca?" Mitch's question came out of the blue. She looked up, startled, sure she was flushing.

"Think?" she echoed. She must have missed their conversation while she daydreamed about Brett.

"About this thing." Mitch had swung himself into the saddle of the machine, and he did an experimental leg raise. "Looks pretty good, doesn't it?"

"Yes, of course." She could feel her cheeks burning. Nonsense. Neither of them could possibly guess what she'd been thinking. Nobody knew that her feelings for Brett were anything but friendship for a childhood neighbor. "It'll work fine, if we can get Alex to use it."

"He will." Brett sounded sure, but again she heard the worry—almost fear—beneath the confident words.

Her heart hurt for him. He wanted so much to help Alex. If he could do this for his friend, it would mean the world to him. His happiness mattered to her almost as much as the possibility of Alex regaining his health.

Please, Lord. Please let this work, for both of them.

The three of them kept at it, and at the end of an hour the room had turned into a reasonable facsimile of a therapy room, complete with mats, weights and workout machines.

"Pretty good," Mitch said, mopping his forehead as he looked around.

"Pretty good?" Brett grinned, clapping him on the back. "It's great. We did it."

Before Rebecca had time to feel left out, he'd flung his other arm across her shoulders. "Trust me—Alex isn't going to be able to resist this."

Maida Hansen thrust her head in the doorway, looking agitated. "He's coming! Oh, Dr. Brett, he's coming. Are you ready?"

"We're all set. Send him in the minute he gets here."

Brett's smile was confident. Nevertheless, she seemed to hear his unspoken prayer. *Please, Lord. Please.*

The three of them stood frozen in place when Maida had gone. Rebecca heard the housekeeper's footsteps on the tile floor as she went to the door, heard Alex greet her.

"Dr. Brett is waiting for you in the conservatory," she said, just the smallest quaver in her voice.

"The conservatory?" Alex sounded startled. "What on earth is he doing there?"

His uneven footsteps came toward them, echoing on the tile. Rebecca held her breath.

Please, Father. This means so much to him.

She should be ashamed of herself, thinking of Brett when it was Alex they were trying to help. But she couldn't seem to help herself. She cared too much. She just cared too much about Brett, and there was no going back.

"Brett?" Alex shoved the door open. "What in the world—"

He stood in the doorway, staring at them in amazement.

Rebecca didn't know about the other two, but her smile felt petrified.

"Surprise," Brett said quietly.

"What's going on here?" Alex moved forward slowly, eyes focused on Brett. "What are you up to?"

Brett gestured around the room. "You didn't have time for therapy. So we brought therapy to you. Now you don't have any excuses. You're going to get rid of that stick, once and for all."

"Pretty decent setup," Mitch said. "Maybe you'll let me come over and work out with you once in a while. It sure beats the barbells I've got in the cellar."

Alex shook his head slowly, his serious expression not changing. Then, just when Rebecca's heart began to sink, the smallest smile curved the edge of his lips.

"You guys..." He shook his head. "I suppose I don't stand a chance, not since you've all ganged up on me, do I?"

His words were so similar to Doc's that her heart skipped a beat. She glanced at Brett. His gaze met hers in a moment of shared understanding before he turned back to Alex.

"Not a chance, buddy," he said. "We've got a whole treatment plan worked out for you, and one of us will be here every night for a while to walk you through it. The only way you're getting rid of us is to throw us out, if you think you can."

Alex's smile grew. "I might manage to toss Rebecca out, but I don't stand a chance against you two. I guess I never did." He sounded perfectly happy about that state of affairs.

Rebecca's tense muscles relaxed. *Thank you, Lord. Thank you.*

Of course they had to try out all the equipment, and then walk Alex through the first level of the program Brett had devised for him. The whole process turned into a lot of joking, reminiscing, and snatches of high school memories.

Not having been part of their high school years, Rebecca could only listen, smiling. A dozen times she thought she should leave the three of them alone together, but she'd come with Brett in the van, so she couldn't just go home.

Brett grinned at her, as if he knew what she was thinking. "Rebecca will be here tomorrow night to give you a hand, then I'll be here the next night. So you're not going to have any excuses for blowing it off."

"You don't need to do that," Alex protested. "I can keep at it myself."

"No chance," Brett said.

"You need someone to spot for you at first," Rebecca put in, before Alex's male pride could be offended at the idea that he couldn't do it alone. "We may need to adjust some of the exercises for the best effect, and we won't know that unless we're here."

Alex's expression said he knew what she was doing, but he nodded. "All right. Thanks."

Mitch glanced at his watch. "Good grief, look at the time. I'd better get moving."

"Expecting a crime wave?" Brett asked.

Mitch punched him lightly. "I'm getting married on Saturday, in case you'd forgotten. I want to spend a little time with my bride-to-be."

"How could we forget?" Alex protested. "Because of you, we've both got to wear monkey suits for the day. I'll look great, of course, but I won't answer for Brett."

That earned him a punch.

Rebecca smiled at their horseplay, but her heart was touched. It wasn't everyone who'd have this close a relationship years after high school. Maybe there was something special about these three. Maybe it was the effect of facing death together and coming out of it in one piece.

The joking continued as they walked to the door. But at the portico, Alex put his hand on Brett's arm.

"Listen, Brett…"

His voice was so intent, so filled with emotion, that Rebecca knew his words weren't intended for her to hear. She quickened her steps, catching up to Mitch with some laughing remark about the wedding.

But her heart seemed to constrict, then expand. It was all right. She didn't know how she knew, but she did. This was in God's hands, and he was working Alex's healing out for his own purposes.

"Don't you have to take the van back?" she asked when Brett pulled into the driveway at his house.

"Not until tomorrow." He slid out, then came around the front.

She opened the door, but wasn't in time to jump out by herself. He caught her hand and helped her down, his fingers warm and firm on hers. He led her to the gap in the hedge.

"After you." He held the overhanging branch back with a sweeping gesture.

"I can find my own way home from here," she protested, ducking through the opening. "I have been for years."

"Yes, but tonight I have to spend a little time thanking you." He followed her across the lawn. "That could take a while."

"That's not necessary." She turned on the step, then discovered too late that the movement brought her face level with his and far too close. Her pulse beat the by-now-familiar tattoo. *Retreat,* her cautious mind cried. But he'd taken both her hands in his, and retreat was out of the question.

"Maybe not, but it's desirable." His voice caressed the word, as if he talked about something other than thanking her. His green eyes darkened suddenly, and her heart thumped so loudly that she thought he must be able to hear it. He shook his head, his eyes never leaving hers. "Rebecca, you..."

"Aunt Rebecca! Dr. Brett!" Kristie whirled out the door in her pajamas. "I've been waiting and waiting for you to come home and tell me goodnight."

"Well, here we are." Brett gave Rebecca a slow smile that disintegrated all her defenses. Then he turned to Kristie. "You look like you're all set for bed."

Kristie nodded, holding on to his hand. "Grandma said I should go to bed early, on account of going to the orchard tomorrow, but I couldn't sleep." Her slipper-clad feet danced a bit on the porch floor. "I'm too excited about the apples."

Brett raised his eyebrows and turned an inquiring

glance on Rebecca. "Apples? What's exciting about apples?"

"Kristie and I are going out to Baylor's Orchard tomorrow after the clinic closes to pick apples. Kristie's never done that before, so she thinks it's pretty exciting."

"And Grandma's going to make applesauce, and apple pie and apple butter, all with the apples we pick."

"Wow." Brett looked suitably impressed. "You must plan to pick a lot of apples."

Kristie nodded, red curls bobbing. "Lots and lots." She looked up at him, head cocked to one side. "You could come and help us, Dr. Brett. Then we could pick even more. I'll bet Grandma would make you a pie."

Rebecca's heart did a little somersault. "I don't think Dr. Brett has time for apple picking. He has lots of things to do."

Brett knelt beside Kristie. "You really want me to come?"

She nodded vigorously. "Sure I do. Aunt Rebecca does, too, don't you, Aunt Rebecca?"

Brett looked up at her. His eyes danced with mischief, and her heart seemed to flip again. "Do you, Aunt Rebecca?"

Do I? I'd walk a mile just for that smile. "Of course," she said primly. "If you're sure you want to come."

"That's settled, then." He stood, swinging Kristie's hand back and forth. "We'll all go pick apples tomorrow."

She was crazy, Rebecca told herself as she said good-night to him and bundled Kristie upstairs to bed. She was just plain crazy. Given what he did to her heart, she should run the other direction, make any excuse to avoid being with him.

What's the point? an honest little voice inquired of her heart. She loved him, there was no getting away from that. That love wasn't going anywhere, because he didn't return it. But she couldn't change how she felt.

And sooner or later—maybe sooner—he'd go away. When that happened she'd be devastated, no matter what she did or didn't do now. So she might as well enjoy whatever time she had with him. It would be over with before she knew it. At least this way, she'd have thoughts of one afternoon at the apple orchard to add to her collection of Brett memories.

Chapter Twelve

Brett could hear Rebecca's voice in the hallway the next afternoon, saying goodbye to Donna Wright, the receptionist. In a moment she'd be ready to leave for their expedition to the apple orchard. But was he?

It had been instinctive, saying yes to Kristie, anticipating the time together. Now that he'd thought about it, he questioned that automatic response. What was he thinking, letting himself be made happy by something as simple as picking apples with a woman and a child?

Bedford Creek was doing something to him, and it didn't have anything to do with his outside life and his career goals. Maybe it really was like Brigadoon.

Actually, he'd thought Rebecca would be the one

to make some excuse when Kristie came out with that spontaneous invitation. For a moment her face had frozen, and he'd been sure she'd find a reason, however feeble, to exclude him.

Then something had changed. He wasn't sure what. He just knew that she'd looked at him with something that might have been resignation in those clear eyes before she'd agreed that yes, it would be lovely if Brett came along to the orchard.

What had she been feeling? He didn't know, and that fact nettled him. He'd told himself he could read everything she thought, but on this occasion he couldn't. And he didn't like it.

He heard her footsteps in the hall, and in an instant she'd swept into the room.

"All right, we're free. The last patient is gone. Let's get out quickly before the phone rings again."

There was so much happiness shining in her face that he couldn't possibly say he'd decided not to go. Besides, he didn't *want* to say that. No matter how much wiser it might be to keep his distance, he wanted this time with Rebecca.

"I'm ready." He closed the patient folder and shoved his chair back.

The phone rang. Making a face, Rebecca leaned across to pick it up. "Bedford Creek Clinic." She listened, then frowned. "One moment, please."

She held the receiver out to him, a question in her face. "It's for you."

He took it, to hear Matthew Arends's smooth

voice in his ear. Instinctively he covered the receiver and turned to Rebecca.

"This won't take long. Why don't you go on home and change, and I'll meet you and Kristie there."

"Okay." She seemed to file the question away. "Don't be long."

"I won't." He waited until the door closed to return to the call.

"Mr. Arends. I didn't expect to hear from you today."

"Just thought I'd check in and see if you'd thought any further about my suggestion. You did receive the material I sent?"

"Yes, I did."

"What did you think?"

He hesitated. But there was no reason not to tell Arends what he thought of the proposal. "It seems very comprehensive. I can certainly see it would be a far more efficient way of providing medical care to the community."

"And have you found an opportunity to tell Dr. Overton your opinion?" Arends's voice was smooth as silk, but there was an undertone of something...knowledge, maybe.

"Not yet. Dr. Overton hasn't been well."

"I understand he's seeing one of our neurologists this week," Arends said.

So he had known. Somehow Brett thought that

little fact wouldn't escape him. "I'd prefer to wait until he doesn't have this on his mind."

"Of course." Arends had begun to sound very confident. "Perhaps Dr. Overton's health problems will precipitate a change sooner than anyone expected."

In other words, Doc's health might make him no longer a factor in the equation. If Doc couldn't carry on, the hospital would get its way by default.

"That may be true." His voice was stiff. "In any event, I can't imagine discussing it with him until next week, at the earliest."

"That's fine." Arends's good humor was unimpaired. "I'll look forward to speaking with you."

After he'd hung up, Brett sat for a few minutes, frowning. Arends was perfectly right in his assumption. Brett thought so himself. The plain truth was that Doc's health problems could force the Bedford Creek clinic into the twenty-first century, ready or not.

In the long run, the community would get more efficient care, care in keeping with modern medical practices. Medicine wasn't a calling or an art anymore, or at least not solely. It was big business, and it had to be handled that way.

That was what he'd been trained to believe. Ninety percent of his colleagues in the residency program would say that. Why did he feel so miserable about the prospect?

One way or another, his time in Bedford Creek

was coming to an end. That made it doubly important that he not do anything to create an emotional involvement with Rebecca. He could hardly back out of the orchard trip now, but he'd have to keep reminding himself they were friends, that was all. Just friends.

"We're here, we're here!" Kristie bounced out of the car, hauling with her the small basket her grandmother had provided. "I want to pick an apple. Which apple can I pick, Aunt Rebecca?"

"Just a second, sweetie. Let us get organized, and then I'll show you." She took the basket Brett unloaded from the trunk.

He smiled. "How long will all that enthusiasm last, do you think?"

"About a dozen apples' worth, I should say." She tried to steel her heart against that smile. "I hope you're ready to do some serious picking. Mom will be disappointed if we don't bring at least two bushels home."

"I'll do my best." He slammed the trunk lid. "Lead me to them."

"You're just like Kristie. Do you want me to show you which ones to pick?"

"I'm guessing the ripe ones." He put his hand on her shoulder with an easy gesture he might have used with Kristie. "Didn't we used to earn a few bucks doing this when we were in middle school?"

Memorize the feeling of warmth spreading out

from his hand. She was going to enjoy this day to the fullest, but without letting Brett know what she felt. That would be disaster, to let him know she loved him.

Create a memory, she told herself as she led the way to the red-laden trees. Then she'd have something to take out and look at in the lonely days after he'd gone away. She wouldn't rail at God, asking why he'd let her love someone who didn't love her back. She'd just take it and go on. That was what responsible people did.

"Okay." She dropped the basket underneath a tree and caught Kristie before the child could scamper off. "We only pick the ones that are ripe or almost ripe." She lifted the child to inspect the nearest branch. "See? This one is just right. This one is too ripe—it's already getting soft. Get it?"

Kristie nodded solemnly, and Rebecca set her in the *V* of a low branch.

"There. You pick just what you can reach from there, okay? Tell me when you're ready to get down, and I'll help you."

She turned, to find Brett flipping open the small step stool the owner had left in the orchard. "I'll go up and do the higher ones. You get the ones you can pick from the ground, okay?"

"Afraid I'll fall?"

He grinned. "You've been known to do that."

For a few minutes they picked in silence, broken only by the *plop* of apples dropping into the basket.

It wasn't an uncomfortable silence; it was the silence that develops between people who know each other so well they don't need to fill up the spaces with chatter.

She leaned back, stretching, and took a deep breath. Any memory she created had to include the smells: the mingled scents of ripe apples, crushed grass, and the faint, persistent aroma of wild mint growing in the ditch by the road.

"Beautiful, isn't it?" Brett inhaled, looking up. "Have you ever seen the sky so blue?"

She glanced up, catching sight of the sky through a tracery of green leaves, brightened here and there by red apples. "Perfect," she agreed. "Clear as crystal."

"Autumn days," Brett said. "I'd forgotten how clear and crisp they are here. As crisp as the taste of an apple." He polished one on his T-shirt and then bit into it.

"You're supposed to be picking, not eating." Her gaze traced the trickle of apple juice on his chin.

He wiped it with the back of his hand and grinned, then held it out to her invitingly. "Have a bite. That's the reward for picking."

She crunched into the apple, feeling the tart juices explode in her mouth. "Mmm. Wonderful." She wasn't sure whether she was talking about the apple or about the way he brushed the excess juice from her chin.

"Aunt Rebecca! I'm ready to get down."

She turned away and lifted her niece to the ground. "You can run around if you want. I think there's a swing in the old tree at the end of this row. Just stay where you can see me, okay?"

Kristie nodded. "Okay. I'll stay where I can see you." She scampered off.

Brett watched Kristie run. "Until I came back, I'd forgotten how much freedom we had as kids. And how much time just to run around and do whatever we wanted. All my friends' kids seem too busy with organized stuff ever to just play."

"It's good for kids to amuse themselves, I think." She dropped a couple of apples in the basket. "We did, and we didn't turn out too badly. I have to admit, though, I'm really feeling my way with this parenting thing."

"Looks to me like you're doing a pretty good job." Brett reached over to toss a handful into her basket. "Kristie's a lucky girl to have an aunt like you to take over for her daddy for a while. Why isn't Angela doing more?"

She found she was blinking away sudden tears at the praise. "I try. Angela tries, too, but she's spending so much time with Ron, planning the wedding. We all felt Kristie would do better here, in familiar surroundings. Everyone here knows and cares about her."

He nodded, stepping down from the stool and

moving it. "Bedford Creek has a way of doing that. Guess that was another thing I'd forgotten."

She moved the basket closer to him. "In a way, I'm glad the tourist season is over. It's fun having extra people around, but it's good to get back to just us." She sniffed an apple, inhaling the spicy scent. "Getting ready for winter. That's a good feeling."

"Sleet, icy roads, snow down the back of your neck, being cut off from the outside world," Brett teased.

"Skiing, sledding, hot chocolate in front of the fire, being cut off from the outside world," she countered.

He grinned. "You might have a point there."

His smile touched something deep inside her, setting up a warmth that radiated through her. If he were around all the time, she wouldn't need a winter jacket.

"I think if I got up on that branch, I could reach a lot of ripe ones," she said, testing the lowest branch of the tree.

"You're not still climbing trees, are you?"

"You think I can't get up there?"

His green eyes crinkled with laughter. "Let's say you'd better wait until I'm in position to catch you."

She hoisted herself to the lowest branch. "I don't need any catching, Brett Elliot. I can do it myself." She reached for the next branch, found a foothold, and swarmed up, surprising herself when she landed on the branch she'd pointed out. She looked down at him, a little breathless. "See?"

His face was tilted up, looking at her, all angles seen from above. "I see you're still a tomboy."

"I'll have you know I haven't fallen out of a tree in years," she said tartly.

"I'm surprised you fell at all," he said. "You always did climb like a little monkey."

She remembered that day so clearly. "I went too high. Then I got scared." She remembered looking down, seeing how far away the ground was, panicking.

"What were you trying to do? See how far you could get?"

"Actually, I was trying to figure out what you were doing. You were over by the garage working on something, and I couldn't see you from my usual perch."

He shook his head. "It probably wasn't anything that exciting. We were always building something, and usually it didn't work, whatever it was."

"I'm glad you were there that day."

He shrugged. "Maybe if I hadn't been, you wouldn't have fallen." He leaned against the trunk. "Anyway, I hope you don't do a lot of tree-climbing when I'm not around. Come on down, now. You've made your point."

She reached for the nearest ripe apple. "I'll drop them down to you."

"Rebecca." He frowned. "Come down. I'm getting a stiff neck looking up at you."

It really did bother him, having her perched on the branch above his head. The feeling gave her a heady sense of power.

"I'm fine." She reached for an apple, wobbled a bit and grabbed the branch. "Or maybe I'm not." The ground suddenly looked awfully far away.

Brett held his hand up to her. "Come on. I'll help you down."

"I can make it." She turned, clutching the branch, and lowered herself slowly down to the next limb. "I'm fine. I—"

Her sneaker slipped, and in an instant she was dangling from her hands. The breath caught in her throat.

"I've got you." Brett's hands were strong on her legs. "Come on, just drop down. I've got you."

He had her. She let go, dropping into his arms.

"You need your head examined, you know that?" But he was laughing as he turned her to face him. "What if I hadn't been here?"

"Then I wouldn't have climbed up there to begin with," she pointed out.

She looked up at him, and their faces were very close. Her breath caught, and her heart seemed to stop beating, then to accelerate so it was about to jump out of her chest. Her lips parted, but she couldn't think of anything to say.

Brett's eyes darkened, his smile stilled. He

searched her face as if looking for something. Then he kissed her.

The instant his lips touched hers, she knew this was what she'd waited for all day. Maybe all her life. Her arms went around him, feeling the strong flat muscles of his back. He held her just as closely, and the world spiraled away until no one else existed but the two of them.

This was what she wanted, she thought. Just to be allowed to love him with an overflowing heart. And then she didn't think at all.

What was he doing? The little voice at the back of Brett's mind whispered with outraged caution. Whatever was he doing? He'd promised himself he wouldn't let this happen. It wasn't wise; it didn't fit in with his plans for his life.

And he didn't care. He trailed kisses across Rebecca's cheek, and it had to be the softest thing he'd ever touched. She felt like velvet, and when he inhaled he caught a hint of lilacs. There had been lilacs in bloom that day so long ago when she'd told him she loved him.

He leaned back a little, looking at her. Her golden-brown eyes shone with sunlight, and her lips, slightly parted, looked pink and very kissable. So he kissed her again.

This time she was the one to lean back, looking up at him with a question in her eyes. "Brett? Do we know what we're doing?"

"We're sure not doing what I intended." He lifted a bronze curl back from her cheek, then slowly traced the delicate curve of her face. "I planned not to let this happen."

Her expression grew solemn. "Why? Because I'm still a little sister to you?" She pulled away from him, and he thought that was a spark of anger in her eyes.

"No." He drew her back into his arms. "Because you're not." He gave up trying to resist and kissed her again.

This wasn't smart; it wasn't what he should be doing. But he couldn't seem to help it.

Something hurtled into his legs, and he looked down at Kristie. "Dr. Brett! Are you done picking apples already?"

Rebecca laughed softly, her eyes shining with love as she looked down at the child. "No, sweetheart, we aren't done." Her eyes met his, still laughing. "We were just taking a little break."

"That's right." He picked up the basket, trying to cover his embarrassment with action. "We'd better get busy and pick the rest of these apples, or your grandmother will be unhappy with us."

He was ridiculously embarrassed. What did it matter that little Kristie had seen him kissing Rebecca? She probably didn't even realize what she'd seen. Or was he embarrassed that it had happened, regardless of whether anyone had seen?

He glanced at Rebecca. She calmly showed Kristie a branch low enough to pick from, and there wasn't the faintest trace of embarrassment in her voice. In fact, she seemed to radiate a peace and maturity that confused him.

He'd always been the big brother, the mature one who showed little Rebecca what to do. Now, suddenly, he felt gauche and uncertain, while she acted as if nothing at all had happened.

The world had turned upside down, and he didn't know what to do about it.

Chapter Thirteen

"Now hand the ring to the bride," Pastor Richie instructed, and Anne's friend from Philadelphia, Helen Wells, produced a gaudy plastic toy ring to stand in for the real thing.

The small group that was gathered in the sanctuary for rehearsal broke up, relaxing the tension of taking part in something both joyful and solemn. Rebecca looked across the aisle at Brett, and it seemed her heart would burst with happiness at the sight of his face. If she'd ever been happier in her life, she couldn't remember it.

"With this ring, I thee wed," the pastor intoned, and Anne repeated the words. Her expression as she looked up at Mitch spoke of so much love that Rebecca's eyes stung.

That was what she wanted. To stand in this sanctuary, hearing Pastor Richie say those words, and to be looking up at Brett with that sort of love in her eyes. The forever kind of love, the kind of love that promised home and children and being together no matter what happened.

She looked again at Brett. Did she dare to hope he was thinking the same thing? During the last few days, they'd been closer than they'd ever been. They'd laughed together, worried together about Doc, worked together.

He didn't look at her as a kid sister now; she knew that. He saw her as a woman—a woman who attracted him. But he hadn't mentioned love.

"What God has joined together," Pastor Richie said, "let no one put asunder." His hands were lifted over Mitch's and Anne's heads, and his cherubic face creased in a broad smile. "And that's it. Do you feel comfortable with who does what when, or do you want to run through it again?"

He glanced from face to face, questioning.

"I'm okay with my part," Brett said. "All I do is stand."

Pastor Richie gave him a reproving look. "The groomsmen support the groom," he pointed out. "You won't know how much your presence means to Mitch until you're the one standing here."

"I guess you're right, Pastor." Brett didn't look at Rebecca, but she was sure a faint flush touched his cheeks.

"Well, that's it, then." Pastor Richie stepped

back, rubbing his hands over a job well done. "Ellie will play the recessional, and off you go. Let's practice walking out, so we do it smoothly."

Ellie Wayne, at the organ, swung into the recessional. Mitch, his arm linked with Anne's, started back up the aisle. Then Alex took Helen, the maid of honor. Rebecca stepped toward Brett.

"Shall we?" He held out his arm, his eyes crinkling as he smiled.

"Of course," she said gravely, and took his arm. They started back up the aisle in step, and a smile she couldn't suppress curved her lips.

It was going to be all right. Of course it was. Even if Brett hadn't mentioned love, she knew he had feelings for her. Surely they had a future together.

Don't be so optimistic, a little voice warned in her mind. *Things don't always work out the way you want, no matter how right it seems.*

It would. She quashed the soft warning. This time it would all work out.

They stopped at the back of the sanctuary, and Mitch glanced at his watch. "We're right on time. Rehearsal dinner coming up next, don't forget." He turned to Rebecca. "I didn't get a chance to ask you before. How was Doc's checkup?"

Probably the whole town knew by now that Doc had spent the last two days undergoing a battery of tests at the medical center. It was impossible to keep something like that quiet in a small town, especially when it was Doc, whom everyone loved and depended upon.

"It went pretty well, I think." Rebecca could hear the relief in her voice. She hadn't realized how tense she'd been until Doc got back that afternoon, safe and sound. "He's been working too hard, that's all. He's under strict orders to take it easier, and we intend to make sure he does just that."

"Glad to hear it." Mitch spoke for everyone, apparently, judging by their expressions. "He's a good man. We don't want anything to happen to Doc."

"He's going to be fine," she said firmly.

He was, of course he was. He'd assured them the specialist couldn't find a thing wrong with him other than that he worked too hard for someone who was seventy-two.

She glanced at Brett. Somehow he didn't look as happy as she thought he should.

In the hubbub, as people found their jackets and bags to leave for the restaurant, she caught his hand. "Is something wrong?" She searched his face. "You don't look very happy about Doc."

"I'm fine." He gave her a quick smile. "I guess I just wish Doc had been a little more forthcoming about exactly what the neurologist said."

The concern in his voice penetrated the haze of happiness in which she'd spent the last few days. She moved a step away from the door, letting the others leave.

"But...he said he was all right. Don't you believe him?"

"Sure." He patted her hand. "Sure I believe him. I wanted more details, that's all."

Doc *had* been a little sparing with the information he'd given them. He'd let her drive him back and forth to the hospital, but he'd flat-out refused to allow either her or Brett to accompany him inside.

"He just needs a little rest, that's all." She looked up at Brett, repeating Doc's words as if they were a talisman. "That's what he said. And we can manage that. There's no reason why he should come in at all next week, with both of us there."

Brett's gaze slid away from hers. "Actually, that might be a bit of a problem."

"What do you mean?" She stared at him blankly. "What kind of a problem?"

It wasn't her imagination. There was something Brett didn't want to tell her. Something he had to tell her but didn't want to.

"I won't be in the office on Monday, I'm afraid. Maybe not Tuesday, either."

Something cold seemed to close around her heart. "Why won't you?"

"I have to be in Chicago on Monday for an interview." His gaze met hers, determined and a little defiant. "I heard from that fellowship program. They're definitely interested in me."

For a moment she couldn't say anything. She could only stand there, staring at him stupidly.

"It's not as if it was unexpected." He apparently didn't like the silence. "After all, it's what I've been waiting for."

What he'd been waiting for. Of course it was what he'd been waiting for. He hadn't made any secret of that. Bedford Creek was just a stop on the busy highway of the life he'd mapped out for himself.

"Yes, I see," she said at last. "It's all right. Don't worry about it. I'll manage somehow."

He didn't look particularly satisfied with that. "I'm sorry, Rebecca. I don't want to leave you on your own, but I had to take the appointment they gave me. If I don't show up on Monday—"

"No, of course you have to be there Monday." She forced something she hoped resembled a smile. "It will be fine. They'd be foolish not to offer it to you."

They'd offer it. Brett would accept it. She watched her dreams disintegrate into ashes. He'd go back on his fast track to success, leaving her and Bedford Creek behind. And somehow she had to figure out a way to live with that.

The rehearsal dinner was being held at a restaurant that was new since Brett's time. He found his way to the side street, perched precariously on the edge of the hill. The Blackburn House sat flush with the sidewalk, its front windows lined with flower boxes. He spotted Rebecca, whisking inside just as he pulled up.

He'd expected to drive her from the church, but she'd slipped away before he had a chance to stop her. And now she looked just as determined to avoid him at the restaurant.

This was ridiculous. Why should Rebecca make him feel guilty? His medical career depended on this crucial opportunity. The timing of the interview was unfortunate, but it couldn't be helped. His whole future was at stake.

He followed Rebecca inside. He had to find a chance to talk with her. He wanted to assure her it would be all right. He'd only be gone for a few days, and then he'd come back and intensify his search for a solution to the clinic problem. If Doc wouldn't agree to let the hospital take over, there had to be a young family-medicine specialist somewhere who'd want the job.

The tiny restaurant held round tables just big enough for the wedding party. Rebecca had managed to put herself between Anne and Anne's friend Helen.

"Here's a seat, Brett." Alex pulled out the chair next to him. It was opposite Rebecca, but she refused to glance his way when he sat down.

Something ached inside him at the sight of her averted face, so familiar and yet so distant. How had she become this important to him in such a short period of time? He hadn't intended anything to happen—but it had in spite of him.

He leaned back in his chair as the server put a bowl of tortellini in chicken broth in front of him.

"Looks great, Jessica." Alex's comment earned a smile from the server as she moved swiftly around the table.

Brett took a spoonful of the soup and lifted his eyebrows. "Wonderful."

Alex nodded. "Jessica's brother is quite a chef."

Brett remembered Mitch telling him she and her brother were dropouts from the corporate world who'd moved to Bedford Creek a year ago to open the restaurant. A risky future, he'd thought, but apparently the one they wanted.

He pictured his own future, pursuing the fellowship in Chicago. It would be exciting, challenging, fulfilling. It would also be lonely until he'd made a few new friends.

Rebecca turned her head to say something to the woman serving her. The pure line of her neck caught his gaze, and he wanted to touch it. To hold her in his arms again.

Who did he think he was kidding? He would be lonely in Chicago not because he didn't know anyone, but because he'd be missing Rebecca.

Alarm bells sounded in his mind. What did he imagine he wanted to happen between them?

He didn't know. He just knew he didn't want it

to be the end between them when he left Bedford Creek. And he had to find a way to tell her so.

"Brett? Something wrong?" He realized Alex was looking at him, realized, too, that Alex had probably said something to which he hadn't responded.

"No, nothing." He turned to Alex with what he hoped was an interested look. "You were saying?"

Before this night was over he was going to have a private talk with Rebecca, if he had to trap her in a corner to do it.

The moment, when it actually came, was just about like that. Rebecca had slipped out of the restaurant first, but he'd been prepared for that and hurried after her. He reached her just as she got to her car.

"Rebecca, hold on a minute. I want to talk to you."

"Here?" She started to open the car door.

He put his hand firmly over hers. "What's wrong with here?"

The others were still inside; the narrow street was silent. Moonlight slanted down between crooked roofs, painting pale shadows on the old brick sidewalk.

She shrugged, pulling her coat a little closer around her. "All right. What is it?"

Now that he had the moment he'd wanted, he wasn't sure how to begin. "About the fellowship...

I want you to understand. Rebecca, I don't want there to be hard feelings between us.''

She looked up at him, her face a pale oval turned by the moonlight into an ivory cameo. "You want my blessing, is that it? You want me to be like Doc and tell you everything's fine."

"No, I—"

"Well, I won't." She swept on, carried on a wave of emotion he wasn't sure he understood. "You always want everyone to approve of you. You expect to turn on the famous Brett charm and have everyone smile. But sometimes it doesn't work that way."

The words cut, startling him by how deeply. "I'm not looking for everyone's approval. Just yours."

She turned away, staring down at the car keys in her hand as if they held a secret. "Don't ask me that now, Brett. I'm too angry that you're leaving."

He took her hands in his, half expecting her to yank them free. But she stood so motionless that only the pulse under his fingers assured him she was there.

"I need to know, Rebecca. Are you angry because you're losing a doctor or angry because you're losing me?" He could hear the strain in his voice. Could she hear it, too?

She looked up then, but it was too dark to read her expression. "I don't think I can separate the two. Either way, you're going."

"Rebecca, I don't want—"

The restaurant door burst open, flooding light and noise onto the sidewalk. The others came out in a chattering group. Before he could say anything, Rebecca pulled her hands free and slipped into the car. In a moment she was gone.

Goodbyes echoed along the still street as people got into their cars.

Mitch stopped beside Brett, giving him a quizzical look. "Something wrong?"

Brett shrugged. "Woman troubles." He watched the red taillights of Rebecca's car vanish around the corner. "You feel like offering any good advice?"

Mitch held both hands up in a gesture of surrender. "Not on this one, old buddy. This time you're on your own."

Mitch's words echoed in his mind as he drove toward home. He was on his own. His future was entangled with his feelings for Rebecca, and he was on his own.

There was someone else on his own tonight. Doc. He glanced at his watch. It wasn't that late. He'd better swing by Doc's house and make sure he was all right.

When he got there, the lights still shone from Doc's windows. Maybe, now that Rebecca wasn't around, Doc would be a little more forthcoming about what the specialist had to say. He strode quickly to the door and knocked.

"Brett." Doc didn't look especially glad to see him when he opened the door. "I didn't expect you."

"Just checking." Since Doc didn't invite him in, he walked in. "How are you feeling?"

"Fine." The testy answer had a slightly tremulous ring to it. "I'm fine. You go on home now."

"That's not very welcoming." Doc could be brusque, but he was never rude. What was going on?

Doc shut the door, then rubbed his forehead with a hand that wasn't quite steady. "Sorry, son. I'm just tired, that's all."

Brett put his hand on Doc's shoulder, feeling the fragile old bones. "That's what you keep telling us. But it's not just fatigue, is it?"

"You calling me a liar, boy?" Some of the old fire reappeared in his faded blue eyes.

Brett met his gaze steadily. "I'm not saying you're not tired, Doc. But there's more to it than that. If the neurologist leveled with me, what would he say?"

Doc stiffened, holding out against him a moment longer. Then he shrugged. "TIAs. That's what I've been having. TIAs."

Transient ischemic attacks—maybe the forerunner of a stroke. It was one of the possibilities that had been in Brett's mind for days.

"Doc, I'm sorry." He patted the old man's shoulder, wanting to comfort him but knowing there wasn't much he could say. "What are you going to do?"

Doc shrugged. "I'm started on meds. Nothing much else to do but carry on."

"Carry on?" Somehow he wasn't surprised. "Doc, you could be on the verge of a stroke—you know that. You've got to slow down and let them take proper care of you."

"No way. I've got patients to take care of. I can't be sitting around, doing nothing."

"If you work yourself into a stroke, who's going to take care of them?"

Doc's face set in stubborn lines. "Leave it, Brett. I'm too old to change my ways."

For the first time in too long, Brett found himself praying for the right words. *Please, Lord.*

"Is that really what you want, Doc? To have a stroke at the office, have Rebecca be the one to find you? Have her blame herself for not saving you, the way she blames herself for not being there sooner for her father?"

Doc winced. "You know how to hit where it hurts, don't you."

He forced himself to speak calmly. "Tell me how you'd deal with a stubborn patient who wouldn't listen to your advice."

"The same way." Doc rubbed his hand over his face and managed a faint smile. "You're right. I know you're right. I just haven't been able to face it. To decide what to do about the clinic."

Brett hated to push, but he knew he had to. "I think you already know what the answer is for the clinic."

"Guess we're out of options." He nodded tiredly. "I guess Lincoln Medical Center will be taking over, like it or not."

"Doc…" His heart hurt. He wanted to make this better, but he couldn't. This really was for the best, whether Doc could see that or not. "People will get used to it. They'll be taken care of, that's the important thing."

"I guess so." Doc sagged into the nearest chair. "Tell you the truth, I'm almost too tired to worry anymore." He looked up at Brett. "You think you could help with the details? Make it as smooth as possible?"

"You know I will, Doc."

"And Rebecca. Rebecca's going to take this hard."

Rebecca would take this hard. And Brett couldn't think of one single thing that would make it any easier.

Chapter Fourteen

Each time she saw him might be the last. That was in Rebecca's mind as she waited at the church the next day. He could leave, and the final words between them would be harsh. Whatever else she felt about Brett, she didn't want that to happen.

She smoothed the silk skirt of the aqua bridesmaid's dress and watched the door nervously. She'd gotten there early, ahead of the bride, to make sure all was in readiness. And to try to catch Brett for a few private moments before the wedding overtook them.

She had to apologize. After a night of agonizing, that was the only thing clear in her mind. It seemed she'd been arguing with God the entire night, and no other answers had emerged.

She closed her eyes for another swift, silent

prayer. *I thought Brett's return was Your answer, Lord. I guess I was wrong. I've tried my best to make it work out, and it hasn't. Please show me what to do.*

Now if she could just resign herself to waiting for God's answer... Unfortunately, she'd never been very good at that. Maybe that was why God kept giving her so many opportunities to practice.

The door swung again, and everything inside her constricted. Brett? No, it was the florist, carrying an arrangement of white mums.

She held the sanctuary door open for the man, and when she turned back, Brett stood behind her in the vestibule. Her breath caught.

Brett, she'd long since decided, looked good no matter what he wore. In a tuxedo, he was gorgeous.

She managed to take a breath. "Brett. I was hoping to catch you before everyone else got here."

He eyed her with what seemed to be wariness. "Did you think of something else you wanted to say to me?"

"No. I mean, yes." She felt the warm flush in her cheeks. "I did want to say something else. Just...I'm sorry for the way I talked to you."

He stared at her for a long moment, his green eyes unreadable. Then he shook his head. "If that was what you felt, Rebecca, you had every right to say it." A faint smile flickered. "Friends ought to be honest with each other."

"I was angry." She shook her head. "God must

get tired of hearing my repentance every time I lose my temper and say more than I should." She hesitated. She couldn't really say she hadn't meant it, because even in her anger, she believed it. She just shouldn't have said it. "I don't want you to go away thinking I'm angry with you."

"Thank you." He held out his hand to her. "Friends again?"

She couldn't hesitate, or he'd think she didn't mean it. She put her hand in his, trying not to let her feelings show in her face. "Friends."

They stood there, hands clasped. Could he feel the way her pulse was racing? She hoped not. But he was frowning down at her, his usually open expression closed.

She had to say something. "Are you... I guess you're taking the commuter flight tomorrow?"

That was a foregone conclusion. If you were flying anywhere from Bedford Creek, you took the once-a-day puddle jumper to a larger airport. She slipped her hand from his, still seeming to feel the warmth of his grip.

He nodded. "That's the only thing that will get me there in time, unless I want to drive all night."

There ought to be a graceful way to get out of this conversation. She just couldn't seem to think what it was. She'd said what she wanted to say, made her apologies, prepared to part as friends. Now the only way to hold on to her composure was to beat a hasty retreat.

The organ sounded beyond the double doors to the sanctuary. Ellie was warming up.

Rebecca gestured toward the sound. "I'd better go. Anne should be here by now."

His hand closed on her wrist again, stopping her. "Wait a second, Rebecca."

His frown made her heart skip a beat. "I really have to go."

"We've got another minute, surely." He shook his head impatiently, a lock of dark gold hair falling onto his brow. "There's something more."

Only the fact that I love you. Her throat went dry as she thought the words she'd never be able to say. She stared at him mutely.

"I wanted to tell you—"

The outer door swung open, and Alex popped his head in. "Brett, come on. Mitch is getting nervous."

"In a second." Brett looked harassed. "I wanted to say—"

Helen rushed into the hallway from the parlor and beckoned urgently to Rebecca. "We need you. I can't get Anne's veil to hang right."

Escape beckoned from both directions. She managed a smile for Brett.

"It looks as if duty is calling us. We can catch up with whatever it is later."

He nodded reluctantly. "All right. Later. But I really do need to talk to you."

* * *

"Are you sure Anne is here?" Mitch started toward the door, apparently intending to check for himself.

Brett grabbed him and grinned at Alex. "She's here, she's here. And they'll clobber you if you try to see her before the ceremony."

Mitch subsided, yanking anxiously at his bow tie. "What do you think? Do I look right?"

Alex straightened the tie. "You look like a nervous wreck. Calm down. You're marrying the woman you love. You can't ask for better than that."

"You're right." He smiled, looking from one to the other of them. "Who would have thought this day would come?"

Brett put his hand on Mitch's shoulder, knowing what lay behind the words. Who'd have thought the boy from the wrong side of the tracks would end up the chief of police, married to a bright, elegant attorney?

"We did," he said firmly. "We did."

It was Mitch's day. He wouldn't cast a shadow on it by telling him about Doc, even though the idea of sharing that particular burden was overwhelming. He wouldn't tell Mitch today, but he had to tell Rebecca—and the sooner, the better.

He'd tried. No one could say he hadn't tried. But he'd been caught off guard when he saw her, and the moment had slipped away.

Later. At the reception, there'd be a moment

when he could have a private word with her. He'd find a way to break it to her gently, although given the way she loved Doc, she'd have trouble with this.

He'd just have to stress the positive. If Doc followed his physician's orders and took proper care of himself, there was no reason why he couldn't have a long, happy retirement. But he couldn't possibly carry the burden of the clinic any longer, and Rebecca had to realize that.

Nothing about this was easy, because there simply weren't any good answers. Only acceptable ones. Well, maybe sometimes in life "acceptable" was the best you got.

Alex touched his shoulder lightly. "Brett? Something wrong?"

He shook his head. This was no time to tell Alex, either. "Everything's okay." He took a second look at his friend. "How about you? I see you're not using your cane today."

"Maybe I'll need it later, but not for the ceremony." Alex hesitated, his lean face grave. "Brett, if I didn't seem enthusiastic about the therapy, I was wrong. And you were right. I probably never would have pursued it if you hadn't pushed me into it. And I can feel it helping already." His grip tightened. "Thanks, buddy."

For a moment Brett couldn't trust his voice to speak. He cleared his throat. "That's okay. Any time."

He'd told himself he needed to repay the debt he owed Alex in order to feel things were right between them. Oddly enough, now that the moment had come, that seemed pretty unimportant. He'd helped his friend. That was what mattered. Maybe he couldn't help Doc, but he'd helped Alex.

Good news, bad news, all piled on top of each other. That was what life was like for a small town doctor. Where you knew people this intimately, you couldn't stay detached. You got to celebrate the good things, like Alex's hope of recovery. But the bad things cut you to the heart. How had Doc stood it all these years?

He knew what the answer would be if he asked Doc that question. Doc wouldn't trade the life he'd had here in Bedford Creek for anything. He'd never wanted it to change.

Unfortunately, change was inevitable. Brett straightened his tie, buttoned his jacket. In another hour Mitch would be married, changing their relationship forever. In a few weeks the town would get used to the Lincoln Medical Center clinic caring for its needs. Change came, like it or not, and usually it ended up for the better.

Would it? A niggling little doubt crept in. Alex could have gone to the medical center for treatment. They'd have provided him with an up-to-date therapy program. But they wouldn't have tracked him down and insisted on it.

Pastor Richie opened the door and winked at

them. "Looks like it's almost time. Everyone ready?"

"You bet." Mitch spoke quickly. "Brett, better get your skates on. You're supposed to be seating people."

"Right." No more time for worrying about the future. He had to get on with the job of seeing his friend married. The rest of it would have to wait until later.

More people than he'd have expected came to see Mitch wed his Anne, but few of them insisted on the formality of having Brett escort them down the aisle. Finally they were all tucked into their pews.

Mitch's elderly friend and neighbor, Kate Cavendish, sat in place of the groom's family, with the baby on her lap and Mitch's foster son next to her, wearing what was probably his first suit. On the opposite side of the aisle, Anne's parents looked elegantly turned out and uncomfortably aware of being out of their element.

The organist swung into the processional, and Brett went quickly down the side aisle to join Mitch and Alex at the chancel. Whatever nerves Mitch had felt earlier had apparently been banished. He divided a smile between his friends, then focused on the back of the church, where Anne would appear.

Rebecca would come first, Brett knew, so he was prepared for the sight of her as she started down the aisle. At least, he thought he was prepared. Then, as a ray of sunlight through stained glass gilded her bronze hair with gold, he realized he wasn't prepared at all. He looked at her, and his heart stopped.

She was beautiful. He already knew that, of course. She was dear to him. He knew that, too.

And he was in love with her.

The thought nearly knocked him over. He was in love with her. How could he have worked so closely with her over these past weeks and not realized it? Why hadn't he known it the instant he looked at her?

He knew it now. She reached the chancel and took her place opposite him, giving him a small, private smile. And he wanted to step right across the space between them, snatch her into his arms, and tell her he loved her, that maybe he'd always loved her, and that he'd never love anyone else as long as he lived.

He couldn't do that, of course. The maid of honor moved into her place, the music changed with a sound like the heralding of trumpets, and Anne started down the aisle.

Only something as strong as the expression on Mitch's face when he saw his bride could have distracted Brett from Rebecca. Mitch looked like a starving man shown to the banqueting table. And when Anne joined him at the chancel, the love shining between them was almost too bright to watch.

Brett's mind leaped ahead, seeing himself and Rebecca standing here together, holding hands, repeating the same vows Mitch and Anne were saying.

Funny that all his adult life he'd run at the first suggestion of anything permanent. Maybe, on some level, he'd been waiting for Rebecca.

"Now, don't forget to try some of the wedding cookies I brought." Rebecca's mother hugged her and then fluttered away, preoccupied with her serving duties. Mitch and Anne had decided on a simple reception in the social room, but that hadn't kept the women of the church from putting together a repast suitable for a royal garden party.

Rebecca hovered near the buffet table, scanning the crowd that filled the room. Brett had said he had to talk with her, and as little as she wanted another private chat, it probably couldn't be avoided. She'd seen Doc come in, but hadn't had a chance to corner him yet to see how he was doing.

Doc veered away from elderly Mrs. Carlson, who undoubtedly wanted to tell him her latest symptoms, and joined Rebecca. She looked at him with concern. He looked dreadfully tired, as if he hadn't slept in days.

"Doc, what's wrong?" She took his arm, drawing him back into a quiet corner. "You look exhausted. Are you sure you should be here?"

He shrugged. "Couldn't miss Mitch's wedding, could I? Guess you've talked to Brett."

"Talked to Brett?" she echoed. "About what?"

Doc looked at her for a moment, then shook his head. "No, I guess you haven't. Maybe he's waiting for me to tell you."

A cold hand seemed to grab her heart. "Tell me what? Doc, what's going on?"

He rubbed a hand wearily across his forehead. "I didn't exactly tell you the truth about what the neurologist had to say. It's not as simple as fatigue. Brett guessed, and he made me face it. I've been having the warning signs of stroke."

"Oh, Doc." The jumble of feelings threatened to choke her. She put her arms around him. "You...but you'll be all right. We'll take good care of you. We will." *I can't lose you, too. I can't.* "What are—"

Doc cut her off with a shake of his head. "Not now, Rebecca." He glanced around. "You've got a reception, and I think I'll just go home and rest a bit. We'll talk later, all right?"

He was right, of course, but she didn't want to let him out of her sight. "I should drive you home."

"Absolutely not." That sounded more like Doc. "I'm fine." He patted her hand. "We'll talk later."

He slipped away, leaving her to choke down her fears and try to paste a smile on her face. She had to get through the rest of the reception. She couldn't let anything spoil that for Mitch and Anne. Then she and Brett...

Her thoughts stopped there. She and Brett would do what? Brett knew about Doc's illness, and he was still planning to leave the next day for his interview. What did he intend to do?

There was only one way to find out. Ask him.

She found him trying futilely to refuse the mound of potato salad one of the ladies insisted on putting on his plate.

"Brett?" Her smile had to look as false to him as it felt to her. "Can I talk to you for a minute?"

He put the plate down on the nearest flat surface, which happened to be the piano. "Let's find a little privacy, okay?"

He took her hand and led her quickly into the hallway. The door swung closed behind them, shutting out the noise of the reception. He turned to face her, green eyes intent. "I thought we'd never get a moment alone."

She nodded, her smile crumpling. "I know. What you were trying to tell me before about Doc...he told me."

He captured her hands in his. "Rebecca, I promise it's not as bad as you might think. There's no reason why he can't have a long, healthy retirement if he just takes care of himself."

"Retirement." She shook her head. "I don't know how he'll cope with that. I know he doesn't have a choice, but I'm so afraid he'll shrivel up and die when he doesn't have his patients to take care of." Her voice trembled, and she swallowed hard. Poor Doc. What was he going to do? What were they all going to do?

"He's stronger than that." Brett sounded as if he were trying to convince himself. "You'll see. He'll be fine, and now that he knows the clinic will be taken care of..."

She looked up, startled. "What do you mean? How is the clinic going to be taken care of?" For an instant hope blossomed in her heart.

"The medical center is taking it over." He said it in a rush, as if he wanted to get it out before she could object. "Look, I know it's not a perfect solution, but we can't wait for perfect. It answers a lot of problems at once."

She grappled with the idea, trying to assimilate it. "But...you sound as if it's all decided. I didn't even know Doc was talking to the medical center. He's always opposed that idea in the past. And anyway, I thought we were too small for them to want."

Brett's grip on her hands tightened. "Doc hasn't been talking with them. I have. They're willing to take over the clinic and merge it with the one in Townsend. Doc can retire and know his patients are being cared for."

"You've been talking to them." This was all too much to absorb. "But Doc would hate the idea of merging the clinics. He's always said Bedford

Creek needed its own doctor. He'll never go along with that."

"Rebecca, Doc doesn't have a choice anymore, don't you understand?" He took a deep breath. "Look, this really is best for everyone. The clinic is taken care of. If I get the offer in Chicago..." He shook his head. "This isn't the way I intended to say this. I wanted flowers and moonlight."

She stared at him. "What are you talking about?"

He touched her face, brushing her hair back gently. "I love you, Rebecca. That's what I'm talking about. I love you. When I leave, I want you to come with me. I want us to build a life together."

The words pierced her heart. She'd waited all her life to hear them. Now he was saying them, but it didn't seem real. It was all jumbled up with everything else that had been happening.

"Rebecca?" His eyes darkened, questioning her. "What is it? Am I wrong? Don't you love me?"

"Love you?" A little laugh escaped her. "I've loved you always. I could never love anyone else."

"Then what's wrong?" His fingers moved restlessly against her cheek, as if he wanted to draw her closer but didn't quite dare. "I love you. You love me. The clinic is taken care of. We can go to Chicago and start our new life. Together."

It was everything she'd always wanted, everything she'd dreamed of all her life, held out to her like a gift. All she had to do was reach out and take it.

But it came at too high a price. Slowly she shook her head. "I can't."

"Can't?" Brett looked stunned. "Rebecca, you don't mean that."

"I can't," she repeated, feeling her heart break in two. "I can't just walk away. Doc still needs me. The people of this town need their clinic. I won't desert them."

His face tensed. "Rebecca, you're not making any sense. You can't manage the clinic by yourself. You've got to accept it. That kind of medicine is gone for good. What do you think you can do by staying?"

"I don't know." Could a heart really go on beating when it hurt this much? "I just know I have to stay. No matter what it costs."

For a long moment he stared at her, hurt and baffled. Then he turned and walked away.

Chapter Fifteen

~❧~

Rebecca stood in the hallway, hand pressed to her chest. It had never occurred to her that the phrase *a broken heart* meant actual physical pain.

She choked back a sob. She wouldn't cry. She wouldn't.

Her treacherous imagination insisted on picturing what it would have been like if she'd said yes to Brett—a wedding in the sanctuary she loved so much, a cozy apartment just big enough for two, laughter and kisses and shoptalk over a candlelit table in the evenings.

She wiped away a stray tear with the back of her hand. She had to sacrifice that lovely image. She'd stay in Bedford Creek because anything else was unthinkable. Too many people depended on her, and she wouldn't let them down. And Brett didn't want this life. She couldn't use their love to try and trap him in a life he didn't want.

She forced herself to look steadily at a future without Brett. Even with so many people around who loved her, it would be lonely.

She took a deep breath. Enough. She couldn't stand here grieving over what wasn't meant to be. She had to get moving if she intended to save the clinic.

No matter how sick Doc was, she couldn't believe he had given in to the medical center.

A change in the pitch from beyond the door suggested the bride and groom were about to leave. Time to force a smile and see Mitch and Anne off on the one-night honeymoon that was all they'd allowed themselves away from the children. Then she'd talk to Doc.

"There has to be something we can do." She paced across Doc's small living room, the silk skirt of her bridesmaid's dress swishing against her legs. "Doc, there has to be something."

Doc leaned back in his chair, his face drawn and defeated, and her conscience stabbed at her. She shouldn't be bothering Doc—not when he was dealing with so much himself. But if she didn't talk to him, who would advise her?

"I wish I knew." Doc made a small, defeated gesture. "This is all my fault."

"Doc, no." She hurried to him, skirt fanning out

around her as she knelt next to his chair. "It's not your fault at all. I didn't mean to make you feel that way. I just want to find some other solution."

"I know." He patted her hand. "But even so, it is my fault. I should have agreed to take in a partner years ago."

"You were waiting for Brett." Fresh pain struck as she said his name.

"No, I was being a stubborn old man. I thought I could do everything myself, and now we're all going to pay the price for that arrogance."

"But Brett…"

He gripped her hand, his faded blue eyes suddenly fierce. "No. Don't blame Brett. He has a right to go where he feels called. We can't make that choice for him, Rebecca. No matter how much we love him."

Did Doc guess just how much that was? Probably. He seemed to know everything else.

But he wasn't going to know she'd turned down her chance at happiness, or why, because she'd never tell him. And Brett certainly wouldn't.

"I still think he owed it to you to stay." She suspected she was beginning to sound just as stubborn as Doc claimed he'd been.

He shook his head. "There weren't any strings attached to the money I loaned him. I wanted to help him become a doctor. If I had other hopes…well, that's all they were. Just hopes. If Brett had come back, I'd have been happy. But I won't blame him for his decision, and neither should you.''

He promised me. That was what she wanted to say, crying like the five-year-old child she'd been. But Doc was right. No one could hold Brett to a childhood promise.

''All right.'' She took a deep breath, pushing down the hurt. ''Forget about Brett. He's leaving. Isn't there anything else we can do to save the clinic?''

''When the clinic board finds out about my health, they'll have to take action immediately— you know that.'' He looked as if the thought left a bitter taste in his mouth. ''And right now, the medical center's offer is the only one on the table. If we had more time, maybe we could find someone, but we don't.''

Time. That was what they needed, what they didn't have. She gripped Doc's hand as an obvious solution struck her.

''What about trying to get a temporary physician? There must be someone out there who'd like to spend a working vacation in a beautiful mountain town.''

''Do you really believe that?'' Doc looked at her gravely. ''Rebecca, think about it. Even if we could get a temporary, which is a big if, we'd still have to find someone willing to take over the clinic on a permanent basis. And we'd probably only have a couple of months at most to do it.''

"You're saying it's a forlorn hope."

"Just about."

She got up, patting his hand. "Right now, I feel as if a forlorn hope is better than none. Do I have your permission to talk with the board members?"

He sighed tiredly. "Tell them I'm behind you, one hundred percent. And, Rebecca—"

She'd started to turn away, but his voice brought her back.

"Don't blame Brett, you hear me?"

She nodded, her throat too tight to speak.

"I thought you might come by." Doc looked up from his desk as Brett opened the office door at the clinic. He seemed to be spending Sunday afternoon as he often did, catching up.

"And I thought you might be here." Brett discovered it was difficult to talk around the lump in his throat. "You ought to be home, taking it easy."

"Plenty of time for that after I retire." A shadow crossed Doc's eyes at the words, but he didn't betray any other emotion. "I wanted to have a look through some of these old files."

Brett suspected much of Bedford Creek's life was contained in those files, if one knew how to read them. Births, deaths, tragedies borne bravely or railed at—all of those and more were hidden in Doc's terse notes.

Doc nodded at the briefcase in Brett's hand. "You about ready to go?"

Brett nodded, unable to speak for an instant. He cleared his throat. "Doc, I wish I could see my way clear to being what you want."

"Nonsense!" Doc barked the word, sounding for a moment like the gruff doctor of Brett's childhood. "This life was right for me, but I'm not fool enough to think it's right for everyone. You've got to follow your own calling, no matter where it leads you."

Follow your own calling. The words echoed in his mind. Before he came back to Bedford Creek he'd been so sure he knew exactly what that calling was. Now...well, maybe now he wasn't so sure.

"I just wish..." He realized he'd spoken that wistful thought aloud. He stopped, then knew he could say just about anything to Doc. "I just wish Rebecca felt the way you do."

Doc looked at him steadily. "You haven't hurt her, have you, boy?"

The words stung him. "I didn't intend to. And if I did...well, she's hurt me about as much."

"So that's the way it is." Doc seemed to understand all the things Brett didn't say. "Well, I'm sorry. I'm afraid Rebecca was born stubborn."

"She won't even consider leaving Bedford Creek." He wished the words back as soon as they were out. He shouldn't tell Doc or anyone else what had passed between them.

"No, I guess she wouldn't." Doc got up, came around the desk and put his hand on Brett's shoulder. "I'm sorry, son. Rebecca's got a pretty big bump of responsibility. Maybe she just needs to be needed. And she's needed here."

Was he thinking that Brett was needed here, too? Was that what he felt but would never say?

The shriek of tires spinning into the parking lot stopped whatever Brett might have said. He turned to the window and saw the police car with Mitch behind the wheel.

"Looks as if the newlyweds are back. Mitch probably just stopped to wish me luck."

He headed for the back door and flung it open. But any joking words about newlyweds vanished when he saw Mitch lift a small form from the back of the police car. Angela stumbled out of the car after him, weeping.

"Kristie!" He reached them in seconds, feeling for a pulse as Mitch carried the child inside. "What happened?"

Doc threw open the exam room door, already reaching for his stethoscope, as Mitch put the child down.

"I don't know." Mitch sent a harassed glance toward Angela, who was crying and clutching Brett's arm at the same time. "I haven't been able to get any sense out of Angela."

Doc grabbed Angela by the arms and shook her. "Stop that at once," he ordered. "Tell us what happened."

The treatment worked. Angela gulped, swallowed and gasped a little. "She was in the backyard, playing." A sob escaped her. "I heard her crying, but by the time I got there, she couldn't tell me what was wrong."

"Did she fall?" Brett's hands moved as he fired the question, assessing possible injuries. If she'd been in the tree house...

"No! No, I know she didn't fall. She was picking flowers one minute..." Angela's tears started again. "I told Rebecca I'd watch her, and now look what's happened. It's all my fault."

"It's nobody's fault." Doc's voice was stern. "Stop blaming yourself and help us figure out what happened."

"I think I know." Brett pushed back the sleeve of Kristie's shirt. "Look at this." The welt swelled even as he looked at it. "Angela, is Kristie allergic to bee stings?"

"I...I don't know." Angela's voice faltered. "Quinn never said anything. Is that what it is?"

"Pale, wheezing, swelling around the lips." He cataloged the symptoms, and Doc nodded. "I think so."

"He might not have known." Doc's voice was low. He glanced at Mitch. "Take Angela into the outer office, will you?"

Mitch nodded, took her arm, then paused. "You sure you don't want me to drive Kristie to the hospital?"

Forty miles over mountain roads. Brett shook his

head. "No time for that. Take Angela out, and try to find Rebecca." Rebecca was the closest thing to a mother Kristie had. She was the one the child would want.

Doc had already prepared the epinephrine. He handed it to Brett.

They worked silently, each anticipating the other's needs, but Brett's anxiety rose. Kristie wasn't responding. There was a bluish tinge to her small face. They'd wasted precious moments getting her to the clinic, more trying to figure out what was wrong.

Brett snatched the smallest endotracheal tube from the cabinet. "We've got to get a tube down her." He moved swiftly, trying not to think of the child who'd leaned against him, telling him how much she missed her daddy.

But a moment later he was forced to throw the useless tube down. "Can't get it. The swelling must have closed her throat."

Doc shook his head. "She needs a tracheotomy. Now."

The words echoed between them. The two men were frozen, staring at each other across the child's limp form.

"You want me to do it?" Brett could hear the doubt in his own voice.

"You're the surgeon." Doc held out trembling hands. "You want to trust these with a scalpel?"

In that single moment, Brett knew why he'd

fought so hard against coming back to Bedford Creek. This was exactly what he'd dreaded since the day he'd set foot in the clinic—the moment when the life of someone he loved would be in his hands.

No choices. There were no choices left. He had to do it. He couldn't let Kristie down the way he'd let Alex down all those years ago.

Guide my hands, Lord. Don't let me lose this precious child.

He took a deep breath and picked up the scalpel.

Rebecca leaped out of the car, not bothering to slam the door, and ran toward the clinic. *Please, God, please, God.*

She hadn't been able to find any other words, not since the call reached her while she was talking to a member of the clinic board. Maybe she didn't need any other words. At a time like this, surely God knew what she wanted.

She ran full tilt into the waiting room and collided with Mitch's solid frame.

"Easy, Rebecca. Take it easy. They're working on her now."

"What happened?" She looked at Angela, who burst into tears.

"A bee sting, apparently. Looks like she's allergic to it," Mitch answered for her.

"It's my fault." Angela sobbed the words. "But I was watching her."

"Oh, honey, I know you were." Rebecca put her

arms around her sister, holding her tightly. "You aren't to blame." She looked at Mitch over her sister's head. "How bad?"

Mitch looked uncomfortable. "I don't know, Rebecca. There wasn't time to get her to the hospital."

"No, of course not." Her answer was automatic. She pushed her sister gently into Mitch's arms. "Take care of her." She started toward the treatment room and opened the door.

Doc moved quickly to intercept her. "Rebecca, it's all right. I promise. We had to do a tracheotomy, but she's going to be fine."

"You're sure?" She looked at him searchingly, heart in her throat.

He nodded. "I'm sure. You can see her, but don't upset her."

He let her go, and she went softly to the table. Kristie looked very small on the white sheet, even her carroty hair exhausted and limp. But the child managed a sleepy smile.

Rebecca stroked her cheek, heart overflowing with prayers of thanksgiving. "It's all right, sweetheart. Don't try to talk. You're okay now."

The sight of the trach tube made her heart stop all over again. It had been life-threatening, and none of them had even known she was allergic.

She looked up at Doc.

"You saved her." Her voice trembled.

"Not me. I couldn't have done it." Doc nodded toward the one person she hadn't expected to see here. "Brett saved her."

Chapter Sixteen

Rebecca stared at Brett, unable to find any words. If he hadn't been here at the right moment...well, it didn't bear thinking about.

"I'll go talk to Angela," Doc said, and the door closed behind him.

"You—" She stopped, swallowed, and started again. "You saved her life. If you hadn't been here..."

"Don't. Don't start imagining things." He sent a warning glance toward Kristie, but she'd drifted safely off to sleep. "She's fine, that's what counts."

"I should have been there." She blinked away the tears that welled in spite of her best efforts to suppress them. "I didn't even know she was allergic. If I'd been there, at least I'd have known what to do."

Brett raised an eyebrow. "Do you want to get

into a contest with Angela about whose fault it is? Make sense, Rebecca. It's nobody's fault. No one knew. Now that you know, you can take precautions. But don't start blaming yourself for something that was pure accident.''

His tart common sense dried up her tears better than sympathy would have. "You're right. I know." She looked down at the sleeping child, and her heart contracted with love. "I guess I just want to make everything perfect for her."

Brett came to stand on the opposite side of the table. He adjusted the blanket gently. "You can't do that, and even if you could, it wouldn't be good for her. You can't play God in the lives of people you love, Rebecca."

"I'm not trying to take over for God." The anger that flared surprised her. She'd thought she was past being angry with Brett. "I just want what's best for everyone."

"And are you so sure you know what that is?" His normally expressive face didn't give anything away this time. He might have been talking about Kristie, but he might also have been talking about himself.

"No." The anger slid away as she thought of everything that had happened in the past few days. "No, I'm not sure." She looked at him. "But I still have to go on doing what I think is right."

"Staying here. Trying to save the clinic." Emotion flickered in his eyes. "No matter how futile it is."

She crossed her arms, hugging herself to keep the pain away. They were right back where they'd been. Probably nothing could bridge that chasm now.

"I'm not ready to give up yet," she said. "We're trying to get a temporary to fill in while we look for someone to take over the practice."

He looked at her intently. "Is that really what you want?"

"Not just me. That's what Doc wants, too."

She thought another spasm of pain crossed his face at Doc's name, but she couldn't be sure. He turned away, face averted, and picked up his jacket.

"Then I wish you luck, Rebecca. I hope you find someone."

He was going, and there was nothing she could do to stop him. She tried to find the words that would let her say goodbye without falling apart.

"Have a good flight." She tried to smile, but the effort failed.

Brett glanced at his watch. "I'm afraid it's too late for that. The commuter's already gone."

He'd missed his flight to the interview that would take him away from them, and all because he'd been needed here. But he didn't seem to appreciate the irony.

"What will you do?"

He shrugged. "Drive through to Pittsburgh and

try to pick up a flight. If I can't, I'll just have to keep driving and hope I can make it in time.''

"But you can't—"

"Sure I can." He glanced at Kristie. "Take good care of her. And of yourself." He pushed the door open and was gone.

It was Wednesday, and Brett had neither returned nor called. Rebecca frowned at the sheaf of papers on her desk—leads to a possible temporary physician for the clinic. Well, Brett didn't have to stay in touch with them. They didn't have any claim on him.

Pain clutched her heart. She ought to have gotten used to it by this time, but she hadn't. It was still just as sharp as the moment she'd told him she couldn't go with him. And tears welled just as readily. She blinked fiercely, willing them back.

"How is it coming?" Doc poked his head in the door, looking at her questioningly.

"It's coming." She closed the folder. There was no point in telling Doc just how slowly. "What are you doing here? I thought you were taking the afternoon off."

She and Doc between them had hammered out an agreement. He came in mornings only; she handled the routine cases as much as possible; and anything that looked serious was sent to the clinic in Henderson. It seemed to be working, but she still worried that Doc was doing too much.

"I'm leaving in a few minutes. Stop fussing at

me." Doc glared at her, but there was no anger behind it, just affection.

"See that you do," she retorted, mock seriously.

Actually, Doc had looked better the last few days. It was as if once his condition was out in the open, the strain had been removed. He seemed more relaxed, and his color was better.

"How's Kristie doing?" Doc leaned against the door frame. "You want me to stop by the house and check on her?"

"No, I want you to go home and take it easy. Kristie's fine. Quinn wanted to fly home, but we told him she's doing fine. We practically have to tie her down. Come to think of it, that might be a good solution for you, too."

He held up his hands in surrender. "Okay, okay, I'm going. But you'll have to take care of the applicant in my office."

"Applicant?"

Doc had already started down the hall, and she had to chase after him. "What do you mean? What applicant?"

Doc shrugged, opening the door. "Young fellow who's interested in the position. Looks pretty good to me. You talk to him and let me know what you think."

"Wait, Doc..."

It was no use. He'd closed the door behind him, apparently content to let her deal with the unknown applicant.

Well, she was doing most of the searching anyway. She'd have to talk to the person in any event, so she might as well do it now and get it over with. And she would not start comparing the poor man unfavorably with Brett Elliot. That wasn't fair to either of them.

Donning a welcoming smile, she went into Doc's office. The person waiting turned from the window, and the afternoon sun outlined him in gold.

"Brett." His name came out in a gasp. She stopped as suddenly as if she'd run into a wall. It couldn't be. "What are you doing here?"

His eyebrows lifted. "The interview's over. I'm back. Did you think I'd stay in Chicago indefinitely?"

"No, I mean—" Her mind whirled, then fastened on to one solid thought. "I'm sorry. Doc wanted me to talk to someone who's here about the position. I thought he was in here, but I guess I misunderstood."

"No."

She stared at him blankly. "What do you mean? No what?"

"No, you didn't misunderstand. The applicant is here. I'm the one applying for the job."

She shook her head, hoping to clear it. It didn't help. "I don't understand. You mean you didn't get the fellowship, so you want to work here temporarily until something else comes up?"

And then they'd have to go through the trauma of parting all over again. She didn't think her bruised heart could stand that.

He shook his head. "They offered me the fellowship. I turned it down."

The words lingered in the air. She considered them, hardly daring to hope. "Why? I thought it was just what you wanted."

"I thought so, too." He took a step toward her, his eyes steady. "I was on the verge of saying yes when something stopped me." He shook his head. "Chicago isn't where I want to be. It isn't where I'm meant to be. I belong here, in Bedford Creek. With you."

"But you—"

With a long step Brett closed the distance between them. He pulled Rebecca into his arms and stopped her words with a kiss.

"I love you, Rebecca," he said. "I love you. I don't want a life that doesn't include you."

She tried to force herself to think rationally, but that wasn't easy with his arms around her and his breath warm against her lips. She forced herself to draw back a little in the circle of his arms so that she could see his face.

"Brett, don't. I can't ask you to make a sacrifice like that."

"You're not asking. And it's not a sacrifice." He lifted an eyebrow. "Or have you decided you don't love me, after all?"

"I love you." The words came out in something between a laugh and a sob. "I've loved you all my life, I think. But I don't want you to make a decision because of me and then regret it later."

"No regrets," he said gently. He stroked her cheek, and her skin warmed at his touch. "Remember when you said you couldn't separate the man from the doctor? Well, I can't separate you from Bedford Creek. And I want the whole package."

"But your surgery fellowship…"

He was shaking his head. "That long drive gave me time to think about things. About why I thought I didn't want a position where I'd care too much about my patients as people. About why it was so important to me to stay detached." His voice choked a little. "I was so convinced God gave me my skills for success. Maybe He really gave them to me so I'd be in the right place at the right time to save Kristie. I've been trying to figure out what God wants for me, and now I know. This is where I'm meant to be."

He drew her close against him, and his breath whispered across her ear. "Now will you please stop arguing and say you'll marry me?"

She was in his arms, and that was the place she was meant to be. Funny, that once they both stopped trying to make things work out the way they thought best, God took care of everything.

She looked at him, seeing the love shining in his eyes, and knew they were both home to stay. "Yes," she said softly. "I will."

Epilogue

"**O**pen one more present, and then I'll serve the dessert." Anne handed a gift to Brett, and he put in it Rebecca's lap.

"Rebecca's in charge of opening engagement gifts," he said.

"Can I help, please?" Kristie leaned against his knee. "Please, Uncle Brett?"

He nodded, drawing her closer so she could help Rebecca undo the ribbon. Colorful paper fluttered knee-deep in Mitch and Anne's living room, echoing the spring flowers blooming outside. It looked as if Anne had invited half the town to their engagement party. His parents had come back from Florida earlier than usual to be there, and his mother couldn't stop smiling.

Kristie and Rebecca bent together over the package. She was so excited about being a flower girl in the wedding that she hadn't been still all day.

Rebecca held the card out to him. "This one's from Doc."

"He didn't need to do that." He grinned at the beach scene on the card. "It's enough that he's coming all the way from South Carolina for the wedding."

"He insisted." Alex leaned across to help balance the package. "He's called me three times to make sure it arrived."

Brett glanced from face to face in the circle of friends as they watched Rebecca open the box. How could he have thought he'd be content any place else in the world?

Rebecca turned to show him the seashell lamp, her laughing face so inexpressibly dear to him, and his heart swelled with love.

"Can you believe this?" she said. "They've practically given us enough to furnish the house."

"Not bad for a woman who planned never to marry." He dropped a light kiss on the tip of her nose.

"Never marry?" She looked startled. "When did I say that?"

"At Mitch and Anne's engagement party. You told me you were content to always be the bridesmaid, remember?"

Mischief twinkled in her eyes. "That's because I was waiting to find Prince Charming."

"And did you?"

"Oh, yes." Her fingers closed over his. "I found him in the doctor next door."

* * * * *

*Be sure to watch for Alex's romance,
coming only to Love Inspired.*

Dear Reader,

Thank you for choosing to pick up this book. I hope you enjoy the love story of Dr. Brett and the woman he remembers as a pesky kid sister. Perhaps you'll relate to the struggle Brett and Rebecca experience as they try to find God's will for their lives.

Have you ever noticed how being aligned with God's will for your life puts everything else into perspective? I thought about that as I wrote this story, but I didn't find the perfect Scripture verse until I taught a lesson to my fifth- and sixth-grade Sunday school class. After hearing the Scripture, one of them said, "You mean God already has good deeds picked out for us to do? But what if we aren't there to do them?"

Yes, I thought! That's exactly the question Brett has to ask himself.

Please let me know how you liked this story. You can reach me c/o Steeple Hill Books, 300 East 42nd St., New York, NY 10017.

Best Wishes,

Marta Perry